Born in Meknès, Morocco, in 1958, **Abdelilah Hamdouchi** is one of
the first writers of police fiction in Arabic and a prolific, award-winning
screenwriter of police thrillers. Many of his works, including the
acclaimed *The Final Bet*, address democracy and human rights issues.
He lives in Rabat, Morocco.

Translator **Jonathan Smolin** is the author of the critically acclaimed
Moroccan Noir: Police, Crime, and Politics in Popular Culture (2013). He lives
in Hanover, NH.

Whitefly

Abdelilah Hamdouchi

Translated by
Jonathan Smolin

hoopoe
AN IMPRINT OF AUC PRESS

First published in 2016 by
Hoopoe
113 Sharia Kasr el Aini, Cairo, Egypt
420 Fifth Avenue, New York, NY 10018
www.hoopoefiction.com

Hoopoe is an imprint of The American University in Cairo Press
www.aucpress.com

Some changes have been made to the English text of *Whitefly*, in collaboration with the author.

The Quranic quotation (77: 1–3) on page 26 is taken from the English translation by Abdullah Yusuf Ali.

Exclusive distribution outside Egypt and North America by I.B.Tauris & Co Ltd., 6 Salem Road, London, W4 2BU

Dar el Kutub No. 14337/15
ISBN 978 977 416 751 5

Dar el Kutub Cataloging-in-Publication Data

Hamdouchi, Abdelilah
      Whitefly: A Novel / Abdelilah Hamdouchi.—Cairo: The American University in Cairo Press, 2016.
      p.   cm.
      ISBN 978 977 416 751 5
      1. English fiction
      823

1 2 3 4 5   20 19 18 17 16

Designed by Adam el-Sehemy
Printed in United States of America

In the good mystery there is nothing wasted, no sentence, no word that is not significant. And even if it is not significant, it has the potential to be so.

—Paul Auster

1

THE RAIN LET UP AROUND three o'clock. Detective Laafrit of the Criminal Investigations Unit approached his third-floor office window and looked out over the boulevard. Bright beams from the sun disappearing behind the rooftops slipped through the two buildings opposite him. The main police station here in Tangier was strangely quiet—the typewriters were silent, all meetings were postponed, and the offices were empty. If not for the security guard standing by the front door brandishing his gun, it would have been easy for anyone to come in off the street and wander around.

Through the glass, Laafrit became immersed in the back alleys. He could see the port clearly between the two buildings when he moved his head to avoid a large billboard. This glimpse of the port always enticed him to follow the boats setting out from Tangier to the other side. Each time, he'd wonder why they didn't shoot this captivating view for postcards since the boats looked from here like they were sailing between the buildings. Laafrit could also hear piercing sirens that drowned out the traffic. They were coming from ambulances, fire trucks, and police cars, exactly like the buildup to the climax of an American movie.

The scene now in Tangier was the real thing. It was in all of today's newspapers. *The Bride of the North* put two huge headlines on its front page: "Hundreds of Unemployed Youth Await News at Employment Office Gate" and "Hundreds of

1

Unemployed University Graduates Organize Protest March." According to reports from informants who had flocked to the police station that morning, hidden hands were coordinating the two groups so they would combine into a huge demonstration marching toward City Hall.

Detective Laafrit, until now, had been spared from the police mobilization. The reason was that he had to finish off an urgent report on a case of premeditated poisoning that had claimed three victims. Laafrit had to highlight the criminal evidence so the file wasn't added to the accidental poisonings that had happened recently in a number of cities, the result of people eating rotten salami. Nonetheless, he was expecting the phone to ring at any minute.

As for Laafrit himself, there was a lot to say. He was a little over forty, had got married seven years ago, and had a beautiful daughter named Reem. He was, to be more precise, of medium height and had a belly that protruded more than it should. His skin was fair, tending to pale, thanks to his incessant late nights. His eyes were melancholic and troubled, with that provocative look you'd expect to find on a cop. It was a look that seemed somewhat ambiguous—affected to a certain extent—but what he was known for most these days was his addiction to sucking on menthol lozenges after he'd quit smoking. His real name was Khalid Ibrahim and he got his nickname "Laafrit," meaning "crafty," from his professional and linguistic aptitude: he was the only cop in Tangier who spoke Spanish fluently and with a remarkable nimbleness, something that qualified him to work with the Spanish police as part of bilateral cooperation to fight drugs and illegal immigration.

When Laafrit reached the crowd of unemployed university graduates in front of one of the trade unions' headquarters, the clash was about to break out. Ten minutes earlier he had received the commissioner's orders to join in. Despite the speed with which Laafrit had driven his Fiat Uno, the commissioner—who was sixty years old, on the brink of retirement, and suffering from diabetes—greeted him with a scowl that revealed his deep agitation. Laafrit had never seen the commissioner like this before. His hair was disheveled, his tie was crooked, and he was looking around wildly, as if he couldn't grasp the details of what was about to happen.

Laafrit sensed the confusion. A quick glance over the scene told him that the cafés, businesses, and shops had all shut their doors and hundreds of bystanders were flooding the middle of the street where the demonstration would presumably erupt after a few minutes. The labor-union headquarters was simmering with the crowd of unemployed graduates. Leading them were protestors raising long banners written years ago, still bearing the same slogans, all of them demanding work and criticizing the government. Only a few meters away, all kinds of police squads were lined up, led by helmeted riot-control officers stroking thick clubs. Other police units blocked off the outlets of alleys and streets. They had instructions to break up the crowd and attack as soon as protestors were ten paces from the union headquarters.

Laafrit noticed that the security forces, despite their confident appearance, wouldn't be able to repel the demonstrators if they decided to confront them. He quickly figured out there were so few men here because the other squads were in front of the employment office. And with the same alertness, he realized the back streets were almost certainly jammed with military vans. He glanced down at his watch, as if he had an appointment.

"I'll try to talk to them," Laafrit said, addressing the commissioner.

The commissioner seemed not to hear.

"I said I'll try to talk to them," repeated Laafrit. "Even if it's just a reminder, I'll make it clear their demonstration's illegal."

"No need for a reminder," responded the commissioner hopelessly. "Dozens of them are law-school graduates."

Laafrit's conviction increased.

"We don't have anything to lose," he said. "If we can calm them down, we'll explain that mixing their demonstration with the demonstration of unemployed protestors without university degrees will weaken their position and diminish their value."

Some interest flashed across the commissioner's face.

"I'm sure most of them have no idea what's happening down at the employment office," added Laafrit.

It suddenly all made sense to the commissioner, and his eyes sparkled. He looked around at the demonstrators and the riot police.

"Go try," he said, increasingly desperate because of the position he was in. "If you bring them back to their senses, I'll owe you for the rest of my life. I don't want to cap off forty years of service with a massacre."

Laafrit took a deep breath, abandoned his provocative expression, and approached the crowd confidently. One of the demonstrators confronted him, but before he could speak, Laafrit patted his shoulder in a friendly way.

"Are you one of the protest reps?" asked Laafrit.

"Yes," replied the demonstrator tensely. "Who are you?"

"Who do you think I am?" said Laafrit, smiling. "One of the cops who tortures protestors?"

The guy had never heard anything like this from the police before. Three more representatives of the unemployed university graduates—including a woman—joined him. Laafrit appeared to be surrounded.

"I came to talk to you voluntarily, as your brother," said Laafrit deftly, filling his eyes with sympathy. "I've also got an unemployed brother in another city. I know what he suffers . . ."

A piercing siren went off in the distance. One of the protestors started chanting a slogan but was cut off by a signal from one of the representatives.

"Are you talking as a cop?" the girl asked Laafrit in a resolute, combative voice.

"I'm talking in the name of the law. Your demonstration is unlicensed. I'm telling you, as your brother, that they'll pulverize you if you take ten steps from this spot. This show of strength you see in front of you isn't a scene out of some movie. I'm not trying to scare you. Out of sympathy, I'm trying to give you advice.

"There's something else you might not know," Laafrit continued after a pause. "A crowd bigger than this of unemployed workers without degrees is in front of the employment office. They came from everywhere to sign up to go to Spain for nine months of farm work. We know from our sources these jobs don't exist—just rumors going around. There's total chaos, smashed windows, and unemployed youth determined to organize a demonstration like yours that'll end in front of City Hall. Between you and me, we've got irrefutable evidence that hidden hands orchestrating everything chose the timing."

The girl's face grew red with anger.

"Fifty jobs in this city were given to people with connections while our association wasn't even consulted!" she blurted out. "Some of us have waited over seven years for a decent job!"

"The agreement between us and the town," said another, "stipulates our candidates would get those jobs!"

"I didn't know this," said Laafrit. "Do you have proof?"

"Names, dates, and positions. Anything you want. They've been toying with our misery. We're ready to put our ribs to your clubs. We don't have anything left to lose."

The commissioner and some inspectors joined in.

"Your ribs are all you have," said the commissioner, commenting on the last sentence. "Without them, you won't be able to work, even if jobs are plentiful."

His comment elicited a few smiles. The commissioner sensed he was beginning to get a grip on the situation and was encouraged to keep going.

"Listen, if what you say about shady hirings is true, I'm ready right now to guarantee you a meeting with the prefect. But only if you put an end to this demonstration."

"Give us a minute, okay?" one of the representatives interrupted.

The commissioner opened his arms wide in agreement.

The deliberations lasted for more than fifteen minutes, and afterward the representatives of the university graduates came back.

"We demand that the prefect meet us right here and now," their leader said in an official tone.

The commissioner didn't respond. He turned away and lifted his cell phone while Laafrit put a menthol lozenge in his mouth. A uniformed police officer stopped in front of him.

"Sir, Inspector Allal wants to talk with you. He just got a report from Central that another drowned body's washed up near the Malabata shore."

Laafrit was dumfounded. Only yesterday two corpses had washed ashore, one at Ashkar and another near the city beach. And the day before, a body had washed up on the stretch between the Atlantic and the Mediterranean.

The commissioner looked relaxed after he hung up. He straightened his tie and told the representatives of the unemployed university graduates the prefect was waiting for them.

"The prefecture will send a private car for them," the commissioner boasted to Laafrit, as if he'd accomplished a great feat.

"Fantastic," said Laafrit. "Problem solved."

The commissioner patted the detective on the shoulder gratefully.

"If you don't need me here any more," said the detective, "I've got to go. Another body just washed up, this time at Malabata."

The commissioner was silent, as if he were considering what he just heard. All his attention was still fixed on what was going on around him.

"What a time for another body to wash ashore," he said, waving the hand clutching the cell phone. "Damn it! Get out of here."

Laafrit crossed the street to a Fiat Uno bearing the word "Police." He found Inspector Allal sitting in the driver's seat deeply immersed in his thoughts. His lips were moving mechanically, without revealing his ideas or feelings, as if they were working on their own.

At three years away from retirement, Inspector Allal was considered one of the sturdiest characters in the business. But he'd had prostate surgery last year, and afterward he discovered his life was meaningless. He stopped smoking and going to bars, and even gave up watching soccer games on TV. His friends suspected the old Allal really died when he joined a religious group whose followers were government employees, functionaries, and a variety of middle-class types. They called for a modern Sufism that could be practiced in the workplace.

Laafrit sat down in the car next to the inspector but he didn't say anything. It was enough to steal a glance at the small prayer beads sliding quickly and skillfully between his fingers. While waiting for Allal to finish his repetitions praising God, Laafrit listened closely to the police radio. Reports were coming in about the chaos in front of the employment office and the police intervening with force to disperse the demonstrators.

Finally, the inspector's lips formed the last sentence of his invocations. He put his prayer beads in his pocket.

"You called?" asked Laafrit jokingly.

"Of course, and with God's guidance as usual."

"And?"

"And may God free you from sucking on those lozenges just as he freed you from smoking."

This was something Laafrit had heard many times.

"Other than that?"

"Other than that, someone found another drowned body, this time on the Malabata shore, only a few meters from Café Rif."

"Fourth corpse in three days," said Laafrit. "Notified forensics?"

"They might beat us there."

"Start the siren to clear the road," said Laafrit.

The car eased slowly through the crowd of cops and then cut through a narrow street to avoid the congestion. They went up a hill leading directly to the boulevard near the main post office. The road was now passable all the way to Malabata.

"Up till now, we haven't heard about a patera setting out," said Laafrit.

"Not as far as I know," responded the inspector. "But it's strange the patrols were reinforced after the trial of the coast guards who were taking kickbacks from smugglers."

"Add to that the dangerous sea," said Laafrit. "It's crazy a boat would risk setting out. But the corpses just keep washing up."

When they reached the beach, they drove out to the farthest dry point opposite the sandy shore. It was a hill of rocky ground with gaps full of thistles. Despite the wetness of the area, strong winds were blowing sand and pebbles all over the place. The waves made a sound like slamming doors. The beach was empty except for the outlines of some people standing far away, under the wooden awning of Café Rif, which was practically abandoned.

The body tossed up on the beach was a male of about thirty. His features were clear and his clothes were distinctive. He had on a leather jacket with big pockets and dark khaki pants, like those soldiers wear. His shoes were authentic new Nikes, as if the guy had bought them just to drown in them. The corpse was laid out on its back and the tracks where it had been pulled from the water were visible on the sand.

Laafrit turned toward Café Rif and saw the bystanders had taken off.

"No doubt they're the ones who pulled him from the water," said the inspector.

"I hope they weren't messing with the body before we got here," said Laafrit.

Before he finished his sentence, a taxi pulled up and someone from forensics got out. He hurried over with a leather briefcase under his arm. Humpbacked, with a face concealed under thick glasses, this was the shortest cop in Tangier. His name was Abdellah, but when he wasn't around they called him "the Dwarf." Panting, he stopped in front of the body without paying it the least bit of attention.

"All our cars are busy with the demonstrations," he said bitterly. "That bastard wanted to charge me."

"Did you take down his plate number?" Laafrit asked, laughing.

"Of course. I'll make his life hell with the traffic cops. He'll rue the day he became a taxi driver."

Inspector Allal moved away from the two. He snuck his prayer beads out of his pocket and gazed humbly at the sea.

"This guy and the others were duped," said Abdellah, looking down at the drowned body. "Human traffickers take them out from the Atlantic coast and toss them into the Mediterranean just opposite Tangier, telling them they've made it to Spain."

"If it's like you say, other bodies will definitely turn up," said Laafrit.

"Who pulled him from the water?" asked Inspector Abdellah.

"We don't know. Maybe the guy who reported it. There were some people in front of Café Rif but they disappeared as soon as they saw us."

"Don't worry about them. They're just hash smokers."

Abdellah pulled a black camera with a big flash out of his bag and took a wide-angled photo of the body. He took pictures of the face and then shots from the front, side, and back. Laafrit walked over to Inspector Allal.

"God be praised," Laafrit said to him.

Allal quickly put the beads back in his pocket. He seemed to be having a hard time leaving his inner thoughts behind.

"The ambulance is late," said the inspector absentmindedly.

"Why don't you radio them again?" asked Laafrit.

Allal lowered his head and walked toward the car. Laafrit leaned over the corpse.

"No need to dirty your hands," said Abdellah. "They call themselves harraga, the people who try to cross illegally, because they burn their IDs before setting out on the patera so that no one will know who they are or where they came from if they get caught. This guy isn't any different from the rest."

"Everyone knows that," said Laafrit, continuing to inspect the body. "At any rate, this poor son of a bitch and his buddies took a wrong turn. Maybe they had a crooked compass or just some bad luck. They should've washed up in Algeciras. They'd have made it to paradise, even if they got there DOA."

Laafrit finished searching the corpse's pockets and wiped his fingers in the sand. When he got up and looked at the car, he was annoyed to see Allal sitting inside with the heat on.

"I'm not happy with him these days."

"You've got to keep in mind everything that's happened to him, Laafrit. Leave the guy alone."

"All this because he joined that group of Sufis?"

"I myself go with him sometimes," said Abdellah, as if revealing a secret. "There are rituals, like dhikr, hadra, amdah, and banquets. Can't you see I've gotten fat? I used to be weak, but the remembrance of God whets the appetite more than any glass of wine. It bestows tranquility and calms the heart."

The Dwarf's unusual eloquence confused Laafrit and grabbed his attention.

"Are you trying to recruit me too?" asked Laafrit.

"Come at eight o'clock. At least fifty people will meet up at the villa of a rich man for a banquet after dhikr and amdah."

"I can understand Allal," said Laafrit. "But did you have prostate surgery too?"

"This is sheer disinformation, the result of ignorance," said Abdellah, lifting his hand angrily. "The prostate is the equivalent of a woman's womb and by simple deduction, it's clear that just as woman doesn't desire man with her womb, man doesn't desire woman with his prostate."

"Where'd you get that from?"

"I asked an herb doctor."

Laafrit laughed.

"You should ask Allal," he insisted.

Abdellah leaned toward Laafrit.

"We're the ones who caused his depression and made his situation terrible. He knew what we were saying behind his back and this affected him a lot. But the truth is simple. Allal didn't lose his manhood during the surgery. Instead, he saw death close up so he decided to get to know his Lord. He went on the hajj and found what he was looking for with the Sufis. He took the lesson he learned to heart."

The ambulance siren in the distance jolted them back to reality.

"Take off his jacket," Laafrit commanded.

Abdellah looked disgusted. He hated touching corpses, even though he'd been in this line of work for more than twenty years. While Abdellah was hesitating, Laafrit took a long look at the body and, for the first time, had a funny feeling about it. This one seemed different from the others, as if the expression of death had been traced on his face before he drowned. His long hair was knotted on top of his head and despite it being covered in sand, it looked thin, obviously the kind of hair that didn't need a comb. What clearly distinguished him from the other drowned bodies that had washed up this week were his new clothes. They caught Laafrit's attention because they were totally inconsistent with the cheap clothes harraga typically wore.

11

Laafrit took a deep breath. He wasn't sure whether he should pay special attention to the guy's appearance or ignore it, but he found himself bending over the corpse, checking it out at close range. The forensics agent moved away.

"I'll inspect him," said Laafrit.

He took prints from both hands. Laafrit couldn't get the wet zipper of the jacket open, so to speed things up he lifted the jacket over the torso and kneeled down to look at the body.

Laafrit's face went pale.

He let out a whistle. Abdellah came over and also dropped to his knees. He pressed on the corpse's stomach with his fingers and began counting.

"The first one in the heart, the second below the liver, the third in the stomach, the fourth—"

Laafrit didn't give him time to finish. He pulled the jacket and shirt off the body.

"The fourth," the forensics agent went on, "pierced his right side. We can't exclude the possibility it passed right through him."

Abdellah got up, reeling, and pulled out his camera again. While he was taking a bunch of photos, Laafrit lifted the leather jacket and examined it closely.

"It seems he wasn't killed," said Laafrit. "He was executed."

Abdellah looked at him, confused.

"No bullet holes in the jacket."

Abdellah pursed his lips the way he usually did when he didn't get something.

"The killer emptied a gun in him and then put his jacket on," said Laafrit.

"Any more surprises?" asked Abdellah.

Laafrit turned the corpse over and saw his back was unscathed. Abdellah tightened his lips and resumed taking photos.

"This isn't the corpse of a harrag. We're looking at a murder and, most important, it was committed with a gun," said Laafrit.

Wearing a look of exhaustion, Abdellah didn't even try to add anything. He just stood there next to Laafrit as the two contemplated the savagery of death, with the rough sea in the background.

The corpse was rushed to the morgue. When the Criminal Investigations Unit made it back to the station at five thirty, Laafrit had a hard time getting through the corridors to the commissioner's office. They were filled with dozens of people who had been arrested at the demonstrations at the employment office. Some had visible wounds from the cops' violent intervention. There were some children there too, crowded together in a sitting room. They were put far from the offices so they wouldn't annoy the police with their crying. Laafrit stopped in front of them.

"Even they were demanding work?" he asked a uniformed cop.

The cop smiled and walked ahead of Laafrit to open the commissioner's door for him.

"These little shits were pelting us with rocks," he said.

Laafrit glared at them provocatively.

"A hundred lashes on the rear for each one!" he yelled, feigning seriousness and trying to scare them.

The kids' cries turned to screams. The cop let out a laugh, baring his rotting teeth.

The commissioner's office was wide, with a large window overlooking the city's pearly lights. The desk, chair, and other furniture evoked the unspoiled air of Tangier from its international-zone days. Everyone said the furniture should have been in a museum but had been sent to the main police station instead, due to budget cutbacks.

The commissioner stood up abruptly to greet Laafrit, despite his lower rank. Their relationship didn't follow the normal protocols.

"I heard today's drowning victim was shot to death," he said.

The commissioner couldn't hide his shock, and was still in denial about what had happened.

Laafrit swallowed the lozenge in his mouth and gave the commissioner the details. The commissioner kept silent, though his excitement was evident.

"Where'd the negotiations with the prefect lead?" asked Laafrit, taking advantage of the opportunity to ask about the unemployed university graduates, and hoping for some praise.

"I've got no idea. They're still meeting. All that matters for us is that the demonstration's over."

Laafrit relaxed in his chair and rubbed his belly.

"And everyone in the corridors?"

"We'll release some and charge the rest."

"What about the kids?"

"We won't let them go until their parents show up."

Laafrit felt like the demonstrations were ancient history.

The commissioner carefully set his pen on his desk and then quickly brushed it aside. He wasn't deep in thought as much as he was enraged.

"Four drowned bodies in less than three days, one full of lead," said the commissioner, as if trying to convince himself of the situation. "What does it mean?"

"It means we're standing in front of a mountain of work," said Laafrit in frustration.

"What lead should we follow? Smugglers, harraga, or what?" asked the commissioner, his features tightening.

"In my opinion, the two intersect," said Laafrit. "My first impression about the drowned bodies is they're harraga. All evidence points to it, but what doesn't make sense is the one who washed up shot dead. He didn't even look like a harrag since his clothes were new and expensive. And it's incredible the bullets didn't go through his jacket—"

"Could he have gotten mixed up with harraga by accident?" asked the commissioner, cutting him off.

"Hard to say. We've got to wait and see if the sea spits up any more bodies. Pateras only set out if they're crammed with twenty or thirty harraga."

"Does the murder victim look like he's been in the sea longer than the others?"

"Not much."

The commissioner was disgusted and a look of loathing appeared on his face.

"If a boat full of harraga went down, it definitely happened near our shores," he said.

"So far," said Laafrit, who was at a loss, "we haven't gotten any news of a patera sinking."

The commissioner put a hand over his mouth and yawned with exhaustion.

"If a boat went out," he said, "it wouldn't have left from the beaches around Tangier. The patrols are too heavy there. Even the fishermen help us out. But who knows?"

The commissioner let out a desperate sigh that sounded more like a moan.

"I don't give a shit about harraga," he said bitterly, waving his hand suddenly. "I want the investigation to concentrate on the gun. Where'd it come from? How'd it get into the country? Where's it now? I want that gun even if it's in a fish's stomach."

These fits weren't unusual for the commissioner. They indicated his blood sugar was low.

They heard a knock on the door and then it opened. A uniformed cop appeared and they could hear the kids' screams and crying behind him.

"Is this a fucking daycare center?" yelled the commissioner.

The cop was confused and hesitated. He looked over at Laafrit.

"Sorry to disturb you, sir. Detective Laafrit, could you tell the kids we're not going to whip them? They haven't stopped screaming and crying since you left."

2

THE NEXT MORNING, LAAFRIT FOUND the medical examiner's report on his desk, together with a plastic bag containing the three bullets extracted from the victim's body and a description of their trajectory showing the murder victim took the shots from the front at very close range. As for the two bodies from the day before, the autopsy established they died from drowning, just like the first one, which had washed up two days ago. The report posited they'd all been in the water for between one and three days.

Laafrit tossed the report aside. It was hastily written, lacked precision, and didn't shed any light on the investigation. He picked up the phone and called the medical examiner. After the fourth ring, he heard Si Abdel-Majid's voice, indolent as usual and laden with formalities.

"Professor Abdel-Majid from the Autopsy Division."

"Good morning, professor," said Laafrit cheerfully, trying to lighten the formalities.

"Good morning. I sent you the report on the drowned men. There is only one problem. I don't know how the shooting victim wound up with them."

"We don't know either. I'd take your report seriously if it actually helped us develop a single lead—"

"I carried out my job as required," said the medical examiner, cutting him off. "If you had read my report attentively, it would have been easy for you to understand that the murder victim took the bullets in vital organs, except for the one in his side that didn't cause a mortal wound. As for the others, they died from drowning and there are no signs of violence on them."

"That's clear from your report," said Laafrit, annoyed with Si Abdel-Majid's arrogance. "If you would, I'd like an analysis of their stomach contents."

"For the shooting victim too?"

"For them all. Thank you."

The detective hung up quickly so as not to give the medical examiner time to object. He put the first lozenge of the morning in his mouth and then called Abdellah into his office.

It was clear Laafrit hadn't slept enough. He kept yawning and rubbed his eyes, which were surrounded by dark rings. Laafrit didn't like the taste of the lozenge so he took it out of his mouth and put it in the ashtray.

Abdellah came into Laafrit's office with a pale face, clenching his teeth. Laafrit glanced at him and told him to sit down.

"Something wrong?"

Abdellah shook his head.

"My stomach," he said, in a voice interrupted by groaning. "I haven't slept a wink. Every time I leave the bathroom I've got to run right back."

"Allal complained about the same thing," said Laafrit, with a look of surprise. "He asked for permission to go to the pharmacy."

Suddenly he hit his forehead as if he'd just remembered something.

"Did you two go together to the banquet yesterday?" he asked.

"To the circle of amdah and dhikr," said Abdellah, correcting him in a weak voice. "At a circumcision party, I ran into a gentleman who honored us with a banquet unlike any other."

Abdellah forgot his ailment and continued talking exuberantly.

"A couscous you eat with your fingers because of its incredible deliciousness. Afterward, tagines with lamb and plums, then chicken with olives and pickled lemons. We broke up the meal with filali sweets and then had plates of all kinds of fruit. But what gave us diarrhea were the cups of milk mixed with rose water."

Laafrit looked at him suspiciously.

"Okay, I've got other things to do than sit here listening to stories of Ashaab al-Tamaa, the unwanted dinner guest," he said. "Take these things in front of me and add them to the fingerprints. Send everything to the crime lab in the capital."

Abdellah took the bag with the bullets and looked at it carefully. He stared at the medical examiner's report and was surprised to see it was only a few lines long.

"What does Professor Abdel-Majid have to say?"

"When you recover, we'll talk," said Laafrit despondently.

Abdellah's face twitched and thick beads of sweat glistened on his cheeks. He sat pinned to the chair as if something serious was preventing him from getting up. Laafrit looked at him perplexed.

"Sorry," said Abdellah weakly.

He left the office and ran to the bathroom.

Laafrit went downstairs slowly. He didn't notice the greeting of the guard brandishing his machine gun at the station's entrance. The detective stood on the sidewalk and looked up at the sky. It was a beautiful day with a clear sky and light, warm winds. Yesterday's rains had washed off the streets and trees.

Laafrit looked at his watch. It was now ten thirty and nothing was moving in the case except for a lackluster report from the morgue. If things kept going this slowly, Central would send in a special unit to take over. That was the last thing he wanted.

Laafrit thought about going to the café across the street for a cup of coffee but he reconsidered. If someone saw him there, they'd think he was on vacation, and at a time like this. Finally, the black Fiat pulled up in front of him. Inspector Allal opened the door and Laafrit got in, hiding his anger.

"Please don't tell me I'm late," said Allal. "The tank was empty and I had to stop for gas."

Laafrit cringed but kept silent. He knew he needed his assistants today and any tension between them might undermine their work. He pretended to be in a good mood.

"How're your intestines now?" he asked.

"Fine. That banquet cost us a lot," Allal said. "But it was worth it."

Laafrit feigned interest.

"The Dwarf told me cups of milk mixed with rose water were the culprit," he said in a tone filled with derision.

Allal glanced at the detective, but all of a sudden he fixed his eyes on the road as a black Mercedes driven by a man with an ugly face cut them off. Allal slammed on the brakes, which let out a screech. The car shuddered. Laafrit shut his eyes as a kind of madness hit the inspector, who began cursing, almost jumping out of his seat.

"Let's get him!" he screamed. "Do you give the order?"

"No," said Laafrit. "He had the right of way."

Rage dissipated from the inspector's face and calmness unexpectedly took its place, as if he'd outsmarted his nerves.

"*There is no power and no strength save in God*," he repeated several times.

He drove through a number of side streets and stopped to let an old woman pass in front of the car. He was careful to slow down while moving behind a bus, even though he could have easily passed it. Laafrit got annoyed. He thought this meekness on the road was in response to him not letting the inspector go after the Mercedes.

"Stop at the newspaper kiosk," said the detective, irritated.

Laafrit got out of the car, leaving the door open. A few minutes later, he came back with a stack of Arabic and Spanish newspapers.

"Hurry up," he told Allal. "We've got to get to Ksar es-Seghir before noon."

Laafrit flipped through the papers. There was no news at all about the negotiations that had broken up the demonstration of the unemployed graduates, even though the front pages of all the papers highlighted the cops' violent intervention against the crowds in front of the employment office. He flipped through the rest of the papers carefully but found nothing in either Spanish or Arabic about a sunk patera. A strange front-page headline, however, made him smile. Laafrit read it aloud:

"Farming Tomatoes in Morocco, a Disease Curling and Yellowing Their Leaves. Morocco Will Soon Become a Tomato-Importing Nation."

The headline didn't pull Allal out of his thoughts, and Laafrit realized Allal was immersed in his dhikr.

The car slowly approached a street that merged on a terrifying slope with a two-lane road opposite the sea. On the right, tourist hotels with dark glass towers came one after the other, with red-brick buildings between them. At the end of the road, the hotels gave way to abandoned warehouses. The road then narrowed and the buildings receded into empty space: hills on the right and a rocky shore with a rusty sign warning against swimming because of pollution levels on the left.

Laafrit couldn't finish the article about the tomatoes. It was too scientific and full of virus names. It was enough for him to read the sections describing the scope of the catastrophe and estimates on the loss of crops in the Doukkala region, which was just south of Casablanca. He folded the newspaper and put it in front of him. He then turned to the inspector and decided to draw him out of his silence by force.

"What do you think about this catastrophe?" he asked. "Imagine a Morocco without tomatoes!"

The inspector laughed bitterly and then was silent as he passed an old truck that looked like a moving wreck.

"Anything's possible," Allal said indifferently. "Here's Morocco today, a country without fish because Spanish fleets have cleaned out our seas. Thousands of their fishermen make their living off our shores while our children fatten their fish with their corpses."

Laafrit turned toward the inspector.

"I spent last night surfing the Spanish TV channels. No news about harraga or a patera sinking off their shores. You hear anything?"

The inspector shook his head. Trying to hide his annoyance, he asked: "Then why're we going to Ksar es-Seghir? What'll Layashi do for you?"

"It's been a long time since I disturbed his calm little life," said Laafrit sarcastically. "Besides, we don't have any leads. Should we just sit around and do nothing?"

Allal didn't buy Laafrit's explanation. He knew from experience that Laafrit always downplayed what he did, without revealing his intentions. He'd pretend he wasn't watching or listening closely and act like he was distracted. He'd move according to a clear plan but give the impression he was fumbling around.

Half an hour later, the car came up on Ksar es-Seghir. In summer, as in winter, the town was calm and pleasant. It overlooks the sea, which almost swallows it up. It's the closest point in Morocco to Spain, and even on cloudy days the banks of Europe can be seen, enveloped in thick fog.

Laafrit told the inspector to wait for him at a café, which had a wall being repaired.

"Have a mint tea," he said. "We're not doing anything official, just checking things out."

Allal was happy to oblige.

As Laafrit scaled stone steps carved into a hill, three guard dogs suddenly surrounded him, as if they'd been waiting for him. He thought about backtracking, but to get to Layashi's he had to climb a surprising number of steps. Layashi's house was built on a hilltop, as if it were a saint's mausoleum.

The barking became louder and the dogs showed a real viciousness and desire to sink their fangs into him. Laafrit was forced to retreat as he cast about looking for something to throw at them. A rough whistle saved him from this hell and drove the dogs back immediately, sending them into the woods. Laafrit looked up and saw Layashi standing on the roof of his house wearing a short mountain djellaba, waving at him with his crutch. Laafrit rushed up the steps, only stopping after he passed through the open courtyard door.

From a distance, Layashi looked like an old sheikh but up close he had surprisingly incandescent blue eyes, bordered by thick eyelashes. He wasn't older than fifty, though his face, which was covered by a thick, scraggly beard, harbored depressions and wrinkles that had been created not by the passage of time but by the horrors and mysteries of adventures. He had begun his life in the northern village of Wad Law as a fisherman without a port or fish—he worked in smuggling and went to jail for it a number of times. From a historical perspective, he was one of the founders of the harraga business in Morocco.

He greeted Laafrit on the roof, laughing, and embraced him like he was a member of the family.

"You've brought us a blessing, if the cops have any blessing!" said Layashi in his thick mountain accent.

"Your dogs would've torn me apart," grumbled Laafrit, struggling to free himself from Layashi's warm embrace. "Always send them out to greet your visitors?"

"My visitors?" asked Layashi scoffing. "They call out to me or whistle. Thanks to these dogs, I live here like I'm in Switzerland. Even at night, I leave my front door wide open."

Layashi pointed to a mat with a rug and pillows spread out on it. Laafrit found it difficult to sit on the ground. He leaned back on the pillow and stretched out his legs, putting his shoes outside the rug. He wasn't comfortable but he gave the impression he'd just taken a load off. When Layashi began getting ready to sit down, limping because of his artificial foot, Laafrit looked out at the sea so he didn't have to pretend to offer to help.

"I left one of my partners waiting for me at a café," said Laafrit. "I wanted to talk to you alone."

Layashi took a deep breath and stared at Laafrit suspiciously.

"What's the problem? Something to do with me?"

"No, not exactly. The problem concerns us all. In the last three days, four bodies have washed up, the last one shot dead."

Laafrit kept an eye on Layashi's face. He didn't see any hint of surprise.

"We thought they were harraga," Laafrit went on, "until we discovered the last one. So far, we haven't gotten any news of a patera setting out from Tangier or the nearby coast."

"The one shot dead can't be a harrag but the others might be if their bodies were decomposed a bit," said Layashi, freed from the tension that had taken hold of him. "If a boat went out a few days ago and sank in the sea or near the Spanish coast, more bodies might've washed up in different places, or at least they'd start washing up."

"We want to be sure," said Laafrit. "Has a patera set out from around here in the past few days?"

Layashi stared Laafrit in the eyes.

"I assure you," he said resolutely, "no boat has left from Ksar es-Seghir or from the neighboring shores in more than three months. Even before then, these days harraga are arrested before they even get their feet wet."

Laafrit deliberately stayed still. He turned his full attention to Layashi and looked at him carefully.

"Why so sure?" he asked, staring at Layashi provocatively.

Layashi gazed out at the sea and sighed with a frustrated look on his face.

"Want to know? Fine. I've got informants working for me."

Laafrit laughed, not believing a word of it.

"So you're deputized by the government to guard the most dangerous shoreline in Morocco?"

"I don't have to reveal this to you," snapped Layashi with a look of annoyance.

"What's in it for you?" asked Laafrit, amazed.

"Just a good deed," Layashi shot back.

Laafrit bit his lip, craving a lozenge. He hesitated, as if considering his words very carefully.

"You know about all the hash-smuggling activities in the area."

"I don't care about hash smugglers around here or anywhere else," Layashi said, waving his hand toward the sea. "What concerns me are the pateras. I promised myself I'd fight this plague from up here on this hill. What I seek is God's forgiveness. You know my repentance is pure."

Layashi's voice became full of grief.

"If I could turn back time," he continued, "I'd have stayed in my village, making an honest living instead of having to drag this lifeless wooden leg around."

He moved his artificial leg so the detective could see it.

"Why do all this?" asked Laafrit suspiciously.

"To atone for my sins and ease my soul," he responded, sighing as if this confession relieved him of some pain. "This terrible business wasn't around when I first settled in Ksar es-Seghir."

Laafrit shook his head in agreement.

"I know the history of harraga begins with you," he said. "But you repented and you paid the price. You lost your leg and went to jail."

"That gives me little comfort," said Layashi regretfully.

Laafrit remembered Layashi's confession when he arrested him five years ago. The interrogation wasn't difficult. Layashi confessed voluntarily to collaborating with some Spanish border guards. He'd bring them a few kilos of hash and in exchange they'd turn a blind eye to the pateras.

At the time, Layashi insisted he had saved dozens of families from poverty. He boasted that hundreds of harraga now lived and worked in Europe, and sent money back to their families. Some of them even got papers. All this was thanks to him.

Laafrit snuck a lozenge into his mouth, placing it under his tongue.

"That's not what you said during your arrest," he said. "I still remember how you were bragging, claiming you provided a great service to the young people who could escape."

"True," said Layashi. "If I only could've stopped at that golden age. What I didn't tell you then tortures me now. I can't sleep any more because of my sins. Every night I hear harraga drowning and crying out for help, clinging to the boat as I beat them with an oar so they don't tip the patera over. Every night I can picture them plunging into the sea, floating dead, the waves tossing them around. Every night their songs, their jokes, their laughs haunt me. When the lights of Tarifa glitter before their eyes, I can see they think they've made it safely, even though they're really standing at death's door. You haven't lived these horrors, Laafrit. No matter what I tell you, you can't imagine that hell.

"It was like the words of the Sublime," he went on, quoting the Quran: "*By the (winds) sent forth one after another (to man's profit) / which then blow violently in tempestuous gusts / and scatter things far and wide.*

"My heart doesn't chastise me for the early days when people made it to Europe safely. It tortures me for what happened after, when I'd take harraga out on a patera knowing death was waiting for them, when I'd trick them by tossing them out in front of Asila, making them think they'd reached the hills of Tarifa. They'd jump around and shout for joy, while most of them died drowning or when the waves smashed them against the rocks."

Layashi's eyes welled up with tears.

26

"Why didn't I stop when the mafia got more and more into the business and surveillance on the Spanish shores became tighter? I acted against my heart and my mountain values. I went into competition with those bastards who live like parasites on people's suffering."

He took out a tissue and blew his nose.

"I'm prepared to cooperate with you in anything having to do with harraga and human traffickers," he added in a grief-stricken voice.

"So," said Laafrit, returning to a calm tone, "you can assure me no patera set out from these shores in the past few days."

"Not to my knowledge," said Layashi. "But you know from your work nothing's a hundred percent."

Laafrit shook his head in agreement and swallowed his lozenge.

"What confuses me is that the last one was shot dead," he said. "And he didn't look like a harrag. But it's hard for us to separate him from the others since we're not sure any of them are actually harraga."

"Take it from me," said Layashi. "No patera has set out from here. Look somewhere else."

Layashi shrugged as if the situation no longer had anything to do with him. He took a snuffbox from inside his djellaba and snorted from it so strongly his eyes filled with tears. Laafrit gave him a sidelong glance and then got up. Layashi made as if to get up too, but couldn't balance himself.

"Lamfaddal, Lamfaddal!" he yelled out to his son in his thick mountain accent, turning toward the stairs.

He gazed out at the sea as if hiding his eyes from the detective.

"My son will keep the dogs away from you."

The car left Ksar es-Seghir, heading back to Tangier. Laafrit leaned back in his seat and put his hands behind his head. Inspector Allal knew this was a sign that meant things weren't going as well as they could and that the detective needed time to think. The truth was that Laafrit didn't have much to think about since the case was still, up to now, at square one. There wasn't any information to build even a preliminary hypothesis on.

Laafrit let out a deep sigh and looked out at the blue sea. He tried to think about what his wife might have cooked for lunch, but found his thoughts swirling around the drowned men and the shooting victim. What secret was this puzzle hiding?

He told himself he might have been too sympathetic and accommodating to Layashi's spiritual ailments. How much could he trust his remorse? Shouldn't he have provoked Layashi in an effort to learn something new about harraga? Maybe he would have discovered some things about the business no one else knew. But Layashi never said harraga die from anything except drowning. Should he give up on the harraga idea and concentrate all his energy on the shooting victim?

He tried to construct a scenario in which two hash-smuggling gangs exchanged fire in the middle of the strait during a drug deal gone wrong. The three drowning victims would have been the first to jump ship, while the fourth would have been shot dead after torpedoing his rival.

Laafrit then remembered neither the three drowned men nor the murder victim had any ID on them when the police combed their pockets. It was hard to get past the harraga theory, despite the problem of the shooting victim. Did they just wash ashore one after the other by chance? It would be hard to confirm that. He thought again how difficult it was to construct a convincing scenario without any reliable information.

Laafrit felt an oppressive hunger, but at this moment he was craving a cigarette. It had been only three months since he quit.

Inspector Allal knew being silent for too long would give Laafrit cravings. Allal decided to pull the detective out of it.

"How's Layashi?" he asked, clutching the wheel to pull a sharp turn.

"He lives tortured by his heart," said Laafrit mockingly. "He can't sleep any more. Drowned corpses yell out in his head."

"That criminal! If justice had hands, it would have put him to death," said the inspector bitterly.

"Justice," said Laafrit, "doesn't criminalize those who help in immigration. It considers them as only having committed a misdemeanor. Layashi lost a leg in his last venture. He was convicted and went to jail."

"And now here he is enjoying the millions he collected. Where's the justice in that?"

"Layashi's combating pateras from his tower to atone for his sins," Laafrit said with more contempt.

The inspector let out a ringing laugh.

"He assured me no pateras have set out recently," Laafrit added.

"And you believe a word he says?"

"What choice do I have? We've got no other source of information in the area."

"Ask the coast guard."

"If the coast guard had busted some illegals, we'd have been the first to know. What concerns me is finding out about a boat that got away."

"While you were at Layashi's," said the inspector, "I talked to some locals at the café. I baited them into talking about hrig and they all said the border patrols have been reinforced in the area and that boats are counted every day. Not a single fishing boat sets out until everyone on board leaves his ID with the coast guard. Anyone new to the village has to confirm his identity and explain why he came and where he's staying. Because of all this headache, human traffickers have moved on to greener pastures."

Laafrit turned to the inspector, who took his sweet time before letting loose.

"The Belyounech woods are full of Africans who get there through the Algerian borders. There are gangs that specialize in meeting them. The smugglers take them to the Oujda train station at night and then help them get on the coal train arriving in the morning in Fez. From there, the Africans split up so they don't attract attention and get on buses and taxis. They go to Tetouan and then to the Belyounech woods, where they find smugglers who sneak them into Sebta by sea through Fnideq, the Great Wall of China that Spain built to divide us completely from Sebta."

Not wanting to belittle the inspector, Laafrit didn't say he already knew all about this.

"More work for the border guards in the area," he said instead.

"They comb the woods!" said the inspector angrily. "I'm totally against this. Why're we guarding a border that isn't ours? Sebta's a Moroccan city and our real border is on its shores, not at that wall. If Spain wants us to help them fight illegal immigration from Africa, they have to leave their beloved 'Ceuta.' We'd be more than happy to take over guarding our shores there. Same's true for Melilla."

Laafrit knew all too well what the inspector thought about the two enclave cities. Whenever the topic of Sebta and Melilla came up, Allal always got tense. Outrage and feelings of injustice and having been defrauded seized him. How many times had he expressed hope there'd be a war to reclaim the two cities, saying openly he'd be the first martyr to die for the cause? Laafrit wasn't ready to plunge into this kind of discussion but it was hard to calm the inspector down.

"So," Allal continued excitedly, "by arresting the Africans, we're giving legitimacy to the colonization of the two cities. Spain has deluded the world into thinking Sebta and Melilla are theirs. So when they arrest a Moroccan sneaking in illegally, they're tossing him out of an imaginary border. And when they hand him over to us and we prosecute him on the charge of clandestinely leaving the national territory, it's as if we're not recognizing Sebta and Melilla are part of our soil!"

"But as far as I know," said Laafrit calmly, "Morocco doesn't officially recognize Sebta and Melilla as Spanish cities."

The inspector hit the steering wheel with both hands and ignored the road entirely.

"And here we are, falling into their trap," he said bitterly, "when we stop Africans from entering one of our own cities, charging them with the intent to immigrate illegally."

Laafrit wanted to change the subject to something more interesting but Allal's appetite for this subject only became more voracious. As they hit a steep decline ending in a dangerous curve, Laafrit reminded him to keep his eyes on the road.

"And worst of all," added the inspector, practically screaming, "our children are dying in the sea like vermin to reach Spain while the Africans who manage to sneak into Sebta are collected in a transit camp there called Lacamorako."

"Calamocarro," Laafrit corrected.

Because the inspector was incapable of pronouncing the word correctly, he gesticulated wildly with his hands, completely ignoring the steering wheel.

"I don't give a shit what its name is! What's important is they collect these Africans in this camp and take them from there to Spain in groups, smoothing the way for them to get papers. But our children who survive the sea and make it to their shores without drowning, if they arrest them, they toss them back at us like unwanted fish."

Laafrit decided it was time to cool the inspector down about liberating the two occupied cities.

"For the moment, our case is still at square zero," he said, changing the topic.

"We shouldn't hurry," the inspector replied grudgingly. "We need to bide our time until we get the crime-lab report."

"The lab report," said Laafrit, "won't tell us if the drowning victims were harraga or not. That much is sure. And I want to figure out that point before the crime lab sends its results. What's confusing me so far is we don't know yet if a patera set out sometime this week. As far as I know, it's been two weeks since the last one. A Spanish patrol guarding the coast saved all twenty-three on board. It left from Sebta."

The inspector slowed down and shook his head as if dispelling wandering thoughts.

"Why do you insist on linking the three drownings to the murder victim? It's possible the drowned men were harraga and the one shot dead was a hash smuggler. Or some guy on a foreign boat."

Laafrit paused, as if organizing his ideas. "First," he said slowly, "the murder victim didn't look like someone fleeing his assailant. The evidence shows he took the rounds from the front. This means he was dealing with his killer in some way. Second, the bullets were fired at very close range. This proves the intent to kill. Third, the shooting victim wasn't wearing his jacket when he was killed. It was put on him after the murder."

The inspector slowed down until they came to a stop.

"Who said he was knocked off at sea?" Allal asked, as if struck by a sudden burst of inspiration. "Why couldn't he have been killed on land?"

3

ON THE HILLS OF TANGIER, Laafrit called his wife on his cell phone. It was 2:20.

"At the very least, you should've called to say you wouldn't be coming home for lunch," Naeema said, unable to get rid of the sharp tone in her voice.

Laafrit tightened his grip on the phone and gave the inspector a sidelong glance.

"Honey, do you think I could've called but didn't?" he said in a gentle voice.

"Where are you calling from now?"

"We were on a trip to Ksar es-Seghir but we're coming into the city now. How's my girl?"

"Reem's sleeping. Did you eat?"

"Not yet. I'm with Inspector Allal. We'll have to make do with a sandwich and get back to work."

After he hung up, Laafrit leaned back in his seat. The car entered the city, moving slowly in the far right lane. The inspector looked over at Laafrit.

"Where do you want to go?" Allal asked, about to stop.

"What do you think about Moulay Mouh?" asked Laafrit. "We can get rotisserie chicken with fries and a bottle of mineral water."

The inspector shook his head.

"My friends on the night patrols pester him. Whenever he sees a squad car pull up in front of his place, his face turns pale."

"Let's go to Si Bouchta. His sausages are great."

"I got dinner from him two days ago when I was working the night shift. Let's leave him alone."

"Take the boulevard," ordered Laafrit. "Ba Driss owes me. He's got a kofta grill."

Allal shifted gears and floored it. The car jumped, letting out a screech. Five minutes later, they stopped in front of the grill. As soon as Ba Driss saw Laafrit, he left his customers and hurried over, wiping his hands on the apron tied around his waist.

Ba Driss gave them an exaggerated welcome and took their orders, bowing his head. In less than ten minutes, he brought them a black plastic bag full of food and then retreated quickly before they made any attempt to pay.

Before heading back to the station, Laafrit told the inspector to stop at the kiosk to return the pile of Arabic and Spanish newspapers he had picked up on the way to Ksar es-Seghir.

Inspector Allal said he was heading to the mosque for afternoon prayers. Laafrit jumped out at the station and hurried inside, carrying his food. Before he'd crossed the corridor to his office, a uniformed cop at the reception stopped him and told him a woman was waiting to see him. She'd said she was an acquaintance. Laafrit hid his surprise and hurried to see who this acquaintance might be. He found her sitting in the corridor with her head between her palms, rubbing her temples. Laafrit noticed her fingernails were coarse from excessive biting.

The woman stood up and extended her hand to him. The way she tried to avoid looking at him, together with the large black sunglasses hiding her eyes, frightened Laafrit. He examined her closely, trying to remember where he had seen her before. She felt his insistent stare and tried to smile.

"Maybe you don't remember me," she said. "I live on the same street as you. We're neighbors."

"I might recognize you," said Laafrit slowly, "if you took off your sunglasses."

A look of distress appeared on the woman's face. She lowered her glasses slowly, as if preparing Laafrit for what he'd see. He was shocked when he saw the swollen bruise surrounded by a blue ring under her left eye. The detective wanted to ask her to wait so he could, at the very least, scarf down his food, but she didn't give him the chance.

"Recognize me now?"

He nodded haltingly.

"Yes. You're a teacher, right? Please come in."

He hid the bag of food in a metal cabinet between the files and asked her to sit down.

"Who hit you?"

"My husband," she replied, on the verge of tears.

He sat down opposite her, trying to hide his annoyance at this unexpected piece of business. He couldn't put it off since she was a neighbor.

"Why?"

"Alcohol," she blurted out. "He comes home every night after midnight staggering, in a pitiful state. When I try to talk to him, it just turns into a huge fight." She swallowed with difficulty.

"Maybe you've heard us yelling? The whole neighborhood knows."

She began to cry.

"Sir, I'm afraid my children will grow up traumatized by this. Yesterday, I decided to put an end to it but here you see the result," she said, pointing to her black eye. "Look how he disfigured my face!"

The detective shook his head sympathetically. He winced because of the hunger pains in his stomach, but the woman interpreted it as sympathy.

"First time he hit you?"

"He always does it!" she burst out. "He attacks me and hits me, insults me and says horrible things to the kids. I didn't want to come here but I can't take it any more. I began fearing for my life when he started threatening to kill me."

35

"Your husband's a civil servant, right?" Laafrit said, trying not to yawn.

"Yes, he works in the employment office, but since there's no employment these days, he's practically out of work. He spends fifteen minutes in his office and the rest of the day at the bars."

Laafrit smiled. The woman opened her handbag, took out a form, and handed it to the detective.

"Here's a doctor's statement. It grants me sick leave for two weeks."

Laafrit looked over the paper, holding it in front of him.

"How many kids do you have?" he asked.

"A sixteen-year-old boy and a ten-year-old girl."

"Anything in particular pushes him to this violent behavior?" Laafrit asked distractedly.

"Money!" she yelled out. "He wants me to give him my salary so he can drink it all away."

The detective nodded again sympathetically.

"An officer will come take down your complaint in a bit," he said in a shaky voice. "Then we'll send a summons for your husband."

A look of hesitation appeared on her face.

"Could he go to jail?"

"That's for the court to decide."

He gestured with his head toward the door but the grief-stricken woman remained fixed in her seat.

"That's everything, ma'am."

"But he is the father of my children," she said quickly. "I don't want him to go to jail. That'd get him fired. Can't you bring him here and reprimand or scare him?"

"That might be possible," said Laafrit. "Give me your address and your husband's name. I'll send the summons. It would be good for you to come too."

Without taking down the information, Laafrit stood up quickly and led her to the door. He then rushed to the bag of food and took out half the kofta sandwich and a can of

Coke. The small patties of ground meat were cold, with white specks of fat hardened on them, and from the first bite, Laafrit smelled something that killed his appetite. He thought it had too many spices, which were used only to mask the fact that the meat wasn't fresh. After taking a deep disjointed breath, he tossed the sandwich and made do with just the fries.

Laafrit got up with hurried breath and didn't spend his usual minute enjoying the view of the steamers sailing between the buildings. He felt cheated and resentful about his work conditions. People who stayed up all night for the safety of the country and its citizens should have their own cafeteria or get reimbursed for meals while working. Even overtime wasn't acknowledged or paid. The station didn't have a coffeemaker and all of the cops' requests for coffee at the nearby cafés were granted as if they were begging for alms.

The ringing of his phone pulled him out of his depressing wanderings. It was the medical examiner, Professor Abdel-Majid, asking him to come to the morgue immediately. Laafrit put the receiver down and stood looking out the window until Inspector Allal finally got back from the mosque. Laafrit was in a terrible mood. His hunger had frayed his nerves and given him a stomachache.

"Send a summons to the address on the desk," he told the inspector sharply, getting ready to leave. "Tell them to be here tomorrow at three o'clock."

Laafrit slammed the door behind him and went through the corridor with long, heavy steps.

With its peeling walls and wooden doors with missing glass windows, the morgue hadn't changed a bit since Laafrit first saw it years ago. Every door squeaked when opened, as if announcing a new arrival.

Professor Abdel-Majid, the chief medical examiner, wasn't older than fifty but his occupation of "carving up" corpses had transformed him into a solemn man with sallow skin and a crooked back. Thanks to his thin shoes, he walked with silent steps. His eyes were devoid of life. He loved to work alone and hated when cops entered his "sanctum." It was very rare one of them called to stick their nose in his work.

He met Laafrit in the courtyard and led him into the observation room.

"Since you're the one who asked me to come," said Laafrit, "you must have found something really interesting."

"As I mentioned earlier, sir, I do not know how the shooting victim came to us together with the drowned men who are harraga."

Laafrit hid his annoyance at the medical examiner's formalities.

"Up to now," he said, "we're still looking for evidence confirming that they're actually harraga."

Professor Abdel-Majid looked closely at Laafrit.

"I have previously examined some corpses of harraga and the condition of these three does not differ from the condition of the others."

"But if you permit, sir," said Laafrit, using the same formalities as Professor Abdel-Majid, "we have not yet received any news of a patera that has set out recently. And you know these boats do not depart with three or four people on board as if they were in a taxi."

"I asked you to come," said the medical examiner, "to direct your attention to the murder victim. He has no connection whatsoever with the others, whether they are harraga or not."

He led Laafrit to the metal table where the corpses were laid out. They were covered by a white sheet stained with dried blood. After a long pause, as if he wanted to scare Laafrit, the medical examiner pulled the sheet back from the corpses' faces.

"Who among them is the shooting victim?" he asked, as if subjecting the detective to a test.

Laafrit thought the question was strange but he picked out the correct corpse without hesitating. The medical examiner nodded in approval and put the sheet back over the murder victim's face. With the same silent steps, he walked to the analysis table and pointed to a jar containing a dark fluid.

"And these are the contents of your murder victim's stomach. He bid adieu to the world after a tasty meal: salad with extra mayonnaise and seafood paella, topped off with a big piece of chocolate flan for dessert. All this was swimming in more than a liter of red wine."

Laafrit was on the verge of laughing at the medical examiner's strange way of presenting the information, but Professor Abdel-Majid took him by the hand like a student and led him to other jars.

"And now here you are standing in front of the contents of the harragas' intestines. The same food in all three: a mix of vegetables, potatoes, tomatoes, and spicy pepper with lots of bread."

Laafrit was more interested in the actual information Abdel-Majid was giving than the odd way he was giving it. He stayed silent for a moment. It crossed his mind, with some annoyance, that he was the one who'd insisted on analyzing the victims' stomachs, but the medical examiner continued.

"And moreover, I found traces of vomit between the drowning victims' teeth. As for your lead-filled friend, presumably he would have lost his dinner riding in a small shaky boat on rough waters, since his stomach was full to the brim. But he didn't."

"The shooting victim's meal is like something served in a restaurant," said Laafrit, emerging from his thoughts as if he had found confirmation for something that was on his mind. "The fact he didn't vomit might be because he was murdered on dry land."

The medical examiner blinked his eyes rapidly without saying a word.

"We are favorably disposed to this idea," added Laafrit in a formal tone.

"Then you have to conduct an investigation into the restaurants specializing in fish and paella," the medical examiner said, as if giving an order. "You don't have to eat at them. It's enough to ask for a menu and show them a picture of the victim."

Laafrit didn't know whether Professor Abdel-Majid was serious or joking. Whichever it was, his solemn air remained unchanged.

Laafrit asked for a few minutes to examine the victims' clothes again. He concentrated his attention on the shooting victim's jacket. The medical examiner gave him a magnifying glass and shone a bright light on the jacket. Laafrit confirmed that it didn't have any trace of the bullets on it.

Abdel-Majid turned off the light. The medical examiner moved the muscles of his face with difficulty, but despite the effort he only produced a faint smile. Once again he took Laafrit by the hand and led him to a metal examination table. On it was a glass tank full of translucent fluid, in the middle of which was a small coin. The medical examiner opened his arms as if presenting a rare gem.

"And now sir, if you please, I present to you my special discoveries that are of no use to any investigation. I extracted this coin from the shooting victim's stomach. He swallowed it when he was a child and it remained in his body. As you see, the stomach acid dulled the coin's surface."

"Wasn't it dangerous?" asked Laafrit, astonished.

Professor Abdel-Majid laughed for the first time, but with a kind of nervousness.

"You cannot imagine how many of these I have extracted."

Laafrit smiled and thought he might have misjudged the medical examiner. Despite his appearance, which could be hard to digest, he might actually be witty.

Abdel-Majid accompanied Laafrit to the courtyard with his silent, cautious walk, as if he were afraid of stepping on an explosive.

"Please hurry and ID the victims," said the medical examiner. "My freezer is so full I cannot accept any new guests."

Laafrit let out a laugh and shook his hand warmly.

"I hope we get that crime-lab report soon," he said.

Laafrit sat outside the morgue in his black Fiat without turning on the engine. He leaned back in the driver's seat and put a menthol lozenge in his mouth. He needed one to help him collect his thoughts.

At this point, three days had passed since the first drowned body turned up and it had been twenty-four hours since they discovered the shooting victim. Laafrit knew from experience the first twenty-four hours were critical. But here he was, facing drowned bodies and someone shot dead without identifying the victims or the type of the gun. The whole investigation was still only groundless conjecture.

What interested Laafrit was that he had found a way to differentiate the drowned bodies from the shooting victim. Everything he'd done up to this point was for this. But what he was hoping to discover was that the drowned men were actually harraga. If that were the case, he'd be able to eliminate all the random possibilities and just follow leads on the murder. But he still couldn't deduce any real facts from the information he had. The case had holes so big even a clairvoyant couldn't have filled them in.

Before Laafrit started the car, his cell phone rang. As soon as he held it up to his ear, he heard the commissioner screaming as if his tongue were on fire.

"Where the hell are you?"

"At the morgue."

"You were at the morgue fifteen minutes ago. Where are you now?"

"On my way to the station. Is there something new?"

"Yes, very new! Get here immediately."

The line suddenly cut off. Laafrit tossed the phone on the passenger seat and started the engine. The car took off with a screech as it left the sidewalk.

4

LAAFRIT FOUND THE COMMISSIONER'S OFFICE packed with men. There was the chief of regional security, with his well-known elegance and striking features, and all the police commissioners from the area. Each was holding pictures of the murder victim's face, which had been touched up with blush to bring out its normal features. The chief of security was flipping through the crime-scene photos, looking at them from different angles. It was as if he were searching for something that had escaped the photographer's lens or hoping one of the pictures would somehow reveal the killer's name.

Laafrit formally greeted first the chief and then the others. He was confused, feeling as if he were intruding on a high-level meeting. Nonetheless, the commissioner introduced him with such celebration that what he said would have taken up half his case report. Laafrit took advantage of the opportunity to show the commissioner's praises weren't gratuitous.

"I just returned from the coroner," he said with a humility befitting his relatively low rank. "I found the medical examiner's report lacking so I asked him to conduct an analysis of the victims' stomachs."

"We agreed to that." The commissioner cut him off gently, casting a friendly glance toward the chief. Laafrit had surprised him by speaking in the singular, as if he were trying to monopolize the brass's attention.

Laafrit got the hint.

"After consultations with the commissioner," he continued, "we asked the medical examiner to analyze the stomach contents of the drowning victims and the murder victim. It's clear from the results that the three drowned men had no connection whatsoever to the shooting victim."

"And the proof?" the chief asked, moving his hand with the grace of a maestro in the police orchestra.

"The proof, sir, is that the murder victim's last meal consisted of salad, paella, chocolate flan for dessert, and more than a liter of red wine. The drowned men, however, only had a mix of vegetables in their stomachs. The conclusion we've drawn from this is that the murder victim most likely ate his last meal at a restaurant."

The commissioner picked up the phone, dialed a number, and gave an order to get a menu from every half-decent restaurant in the city. As he was calling, a fax came in. He held it up in front of Laafrit.

"We just got information on the gun. It's a Beretta nine-millimeter."

"And the victims' identities?" asked Laafrit impatiently.

"That's all they're working on at Central," responded the chief.

The detective felt the key element in the case was still missing. Without knowing the identity of even one of the victims, it would be difficult to come up with a solid lead on the killer or the motive for the murder.

Laafrit went back to his office and relaxed in his chair. He put a menthol lozenge in his mouth, broke it apart with his teeth, and chewed the pieces slowly. He then got up and stood staring outside distractedly. He was thinking it was time to start using his insider information on Tangier and its labyrinths, gangs, and smugglers. He had informants all over the place. If it weren't for the gun, he would have cracked this case in half a day.

A Beretta nine-millimeter? But the real question was: who'd dare have a gun here in Tangier? Hash smugglers? He went over in his mind all the crazy hash barons he knew, one by one. Their styles just didn't jive with taking that kind of risk. Even if they wanted to liquidate a snitch or protégé or informant, they definitely wouldn't have resorted to using a gun. At the same time, Laafrit knew from the last time they cracked down on big-time smugglers that the police didn't control the playing field like they used to. If the cops took one step forward, the smugglers always took two.

Were they heading in the wrong direction? Laafrit was struck again by how little information they had. He couldn't figure out a way to be convinced that the crime had taken place on land. But he thought it made sense to keep going on this assumption until something else turned up.

The detective leaned back in his chair again and went through his mental list of informants. All of a sudden, the tension gripping him dissipated. He smiled to himself and pulled a phone number from memory. As he dialed it, his fingers began to tremble and he almost forgot what he wanted to say.

The Pyramids was one of the most famous spots in Tangier, a place of real Dionysian pleasure. It had three floors and a basement nightclub that attracted the most beautiful women and biggest spenders in town. On the top floor was an air-conditioned American-style bar. Drinks were double what they cost anywhere else in town and only VIPs could get in. From the bar windows the lights of Gibraltar sparkled, even on cloudy nights, as if it were one of the districts of Tangier.

Fifi, the most famous dancer in Tangier, was sitting in a corner of the bar. Not yet twenty-five, she had the best body a dancer of her age could hope to have. Her blonde hair moved like silk and her eyes were almond colored and hypnotic, emitting temptation. She was wearing a black sleeveless dress and had on the slightest touch of makeup. When she bent her head a little, her face bore the true meaning of pleasure.

She asked Nadia, the bartender, to open a beer for her and then lit a cigarette. Fifi looked at the wall clock that had the name of a whiskey brand on it. It was seven fifteen. There were only two other customers in the bar, and they were sitting at a table next to the window overlooking the sea.

Nadia herself was very beautiful. Her only flaws were a slight fleshiness and breasts that sagged a little. She clinked her glass against Fifi's.

"I almost didn't believe my eyes when I saw you," said Nadia with delight. "Fifi's back! Last time you were with that friend of yours. About three months ago."

Fifi drank half the beer and put out her cigarette in the ashtray, even though she'd only taken two drags.

"I'm waiting for the same friend today," she said.

Fifi gave her a special wink and Nadia understood she wanted to be left alone.

Four strikingly elegant men entered the bar. The maître d' met them with a broad flattering smile and led them to a table next to the window overlooking the sea. In the midst of welcoming them, he looked up quickly at the entrance. All of a sudden, the maître d' called to one of the waiters to attend to the four gentlemen and then rushed over to the new arrival.

"Welcome! Welcome! A blessing has been visited upon us!" he said to Laafrit in a clumsy outburst.

The detective performed the obligatory replies and let the maître d' lead the way to Fifi. The maître d' held her hand ostentatiously to his lips and kissed it as if she were a princess. He then turned and made way for the detective.

"Thank you for bringing Laafrit to us!" he said to Fifi.

Confronted by such a scene, Laafrit couldn't stop himself from laughing.

"Nadia!" yelled the maître d'. "If I see empty glasses in this corner, I'll demote you!"

Nadia moved nimbly, her full breasts quivering. She greeted Laafrit with a slight bow and turned to the stereo to put on slower music. She then wiped off the counter in front of the detective.

"I'm at the service of only you two tonight."

Laafrit swallowed the lozenge in his mouth and asked for a whiskey on the rocks. Fifi ordered another beer.

Laafrit looked at Fifi closely and swallowed with difficulty.

"Thanks for coming," he said in an unsettled voice.

Fifi looked at him, enjoying his nervousness, and moved her face closer to his.

"Thought I wouldn't?"

"No, no, it's just I haven't seen you in three months," he stammered.

Nadia brought the drinks and then gently backed away, as if in apology for disturbing them, even though they hadn't even noticed her.

Laafrit filled Fifi's glass and lifted his own.

"Cheers!"

"Still dancing at Macarena?" he asked.

"Every day," said Fifi. "And Saturday and Sunday at Club East. But why're you asking? You know where I dance."

Laafrit kept silent, staring at her lips. It was hard for him to ignore her seductive delicacy, burning sensuality, and penetrating scent. She was sitting enticingly on the barstool. Her soft, supple shoulders emanated tenderness and her hand, with its long polished nails, was moving in a steady rhythm as she lifted the glass to her lips.

Laafrit was irritated at his weakness, so to regain his self-control he reminded himself of when she was in front of him, crying and kissing his hand, begging for mercy. That was three years ago at the Golden Castle, the private club for human traffickers, hash barons, and big-time traffickers. On that night alone, Fifi had raked in three grand on the dance floor and somehow brought down a millionaire smuggler who insulted her when he told her to pick up a wad of cash from the floor "with her ass." As soon as Fifi's escort heard that, he pulled a knife and plunged it into the smuggler's stomach. During the investigation, Laafrit was shocked by the incredible treasure trove of information she gave him about dealers, hash barons, and human traffickers. After negotiations with the commissioner, he decided to release her, on the condition she worked as an informant. But Laafrit, now intoxicated by her beauty, thought she would've been better cast as a spy in a James Bond movie.

Laafrit faced her and struggled not to drown in her deeply seductive eyes.

"I know you dance at Scheherazade tonight," he whispered firmly.

"You're a cop," she said in a low voice, winking at him, "but I don't know why you guys beat around the bush about every little thing instead of just saying what's on your mind."

Laafrit finished his drink in two gulps. As soon as he put the glass on the counter, Nadia rushed to refill it.

"It's the business," confessed Laafrit, smiling. "We play dumb to make the other guy feel smart. That way he offers up what he knows."

"Strange," said Fifi, biting her lip. "I thought it was because you were attracted to me. Why don't you come see me dance tonight? There won't be anyone in the club except tourists."

"There's a conference, right?"

"Not exactly," she said disdainfully. "A group of Spanish businessmen came here to invest in Tangier, if you know what I mean."

Fifi let out an insolent laugh that didn't amuse Laafrit.

"That reminds me," she added. "What's new with Luis? Are you in touch?"

"He's fine," Laafrit replied tersely.

The detective gave her a moment as she drained half her glass. He then leaned toward her.

"I asked you to come because I need you," he said discreetly.

Fifi pulled away and looked at him carefully. Laafrit cast a glance around him and leaned over his drink. He took a sip and rolled the whiskey around his mouth for a moment before swallowing.

"Heard of any pateras setting out recently?" he asked.

Her lovely hand took a pack of cigarettes out of a purse that probably cost as much as Laafrit's monthly salary. She put a cigarette between her lips and waited for the detective to light it, but Laafrit didn't move. Fifi smiled at him, perplexed.

"Human traffickers aren't welcome at discos or nightclubs any more," she said. "Their golden age is over, especially in this area. These days, hrig's bustling in Sebta."

Laafrit lit the cigarette for her.

"What do you have on Sebta?" he asked, taking a sip from his glass.

"Interested in what goes on there?"

"Tell me what you know and we'll see."

"Last week, I was with Essabtawi," revealed Fifi.

"You mean with Wald Lakbira?" said Laafrit, surprised.

She nodded and took a few sips from her glass without the least bit of enjoyment.

"He scored big time," she said, almost bragging. "He made it past the coast guard on a patera with thirty harraga. They all got to Spain safely except for three or four who drowned."

Laafrit finished off his drink in a single gulp. Nadia suddenly appeared in front of them and took the glasses and the empty bottle of beer. Fifi stopped her.

"No more beer for me. I'll have a whiskey."

Laafrit tensed up. Despite the stiff drink, he needed one of his menthol lozenges to get a grip on his nerves.

"Wald Lakbira's still in Tangier?"

"He spent two days with me and went back to Sebta," she said.

"You sure about the number of drowned he told you about?"

"I told you: three or four. Even he doesn't know for sure."

49

Laafrit fell silent. He wondered if the bodies that washed up in Tangier could be the same ones Wald Lakbira had told Fifi about. How much distance would a corpse have to cover between Sebta and Tangier?

Nadia brought the drinks and left. Laafrit and Fifi were speaking so seriously Nadia thought there wasn't much affection between them. For his part, Laafrit knew his dry style was clashing with Fifi's delicacy. He was treating her like she was a man.

Laafrit let out a laugh, wrapped his arm around her, and squeezed her tender forearm. Fifi was taken by surprise and stared at him, confused.

"Let's try to act natural," he said. "We don't want to attract attention."

She let out a laugh, but pretended to be upset when Laafrit took his hand off her.

"Put it back!" she gasped, feigning protest.

Laafrit couldn't stop himself from laughing. How sweet it was to embrace this warm gazelle. If he kept this up, Laafrit knew, he wouldn't be able to resist her. He took a gulp from his glass and went back to work, trying to keep up as relaxed an appearance as possible.

"Does Wald Lakbira have a piece?"

Fifi shook her head.

"What do you mean? A gun?"

"Yeah."

"I don't know."

"Does he have a place here in Tangier?"

She shook her head again.

"Where does he stay when he comes to town?"

"At posh hotels."

"Ever notice any kind of weapon on him?"

Fifi hesitated, then said: "He has a special kind of knife and a small electrified club that can paralyze someone."

Laafrit looked at her insistently.

"Who did Wald Lakbira meet with when he was here in Tangier?"

She took a small sip from her glass.

"He visited his aunt in Marshan and gave her some money. He spent the rest of his time with me. As I said, he was only here two days."

"You were together even during the day?" Laafrit pressed.

Fifi laughed.

"We were up all night and spent the day sleeping," she revealed with a coy smile.

Laafrit stayed silent and gave her a cold look. A sudden feeling of jealousy erupted from deep within. He found himself imagining what Fifi would look like if she stripped off her clothes. He realized he was forgetting work and getting dangerously close to her. He wondered if he would respond to the appeal of her eyes or keep his desire under wraps. As if she wanted to help him decide, she pushed her thigh forward and rested it on his. A sweet ache he'd never experienced before reverberated through his body. Laafrit knew if he kept sitting there and drinking whiskey like that, he'd definitely cave in. He decided to pull himself back and return to reason.

"You're real close with most of the big shots here in Tangier," he said, moving his thigh away gently. "You've been to their houses and danced at their private parties. In all this time, did you ever see something like a firearm or gun at their places?"

Fifi kept quiet for a few seconds and looked at Laafrit cautiously. She shrugged and took out another cigarette. This time, Laafrit lit it instantly. Looking somber, Fifi took a deep breath and finally shook her head.

"No."

"You sure?"

"Don't press me, please," she said nervously. "You know I'm never stingy with help."

The temperature was rising in the bar as more customers came in. Nadia changed the music to something livelier. She took a quick look at the two sitting in the corner and moved to the other side of the bar. Nadia sat with a guy at the counter, trying to distract him from paying too much attention to Fifi.

Laafrit wrapped his arm around her again.

"A body just washed ashore . . . shot dead," he whispered softly in her ear.

She pulled away from him.

"When?" she asked, astonished.

"Yesterday."

"Is that why there are so many patrols in the streets?" she asked, crossing her legs. "I danced for only ten people yesterday."

"It's best you take a vacation," said Laafrit, only half joking. "The situation won't calm down until we have that gun."

Fifi sat up suddenly with a cryptic expression on her face. She stared Laafrit in the eye as if she were afraid to speak.

"Remember something?" he asked, louder than he should have.

"I don't know," she said, collecting her thoughts. "Maybe I did hear something about a gun."

Laafrit straightened up, face twitching. He thought it was better not to interrupt.

"You know Faouzia? The girl they arrested doped up on pills?"

"Yeah, you asked me to let her off," said Laafrit, cutting her short impatiently.

"She emigrated to Italy last month on a fake passport."

"You said you'd heard something about a gun," said Laafrit, quickly pulling her back to what he was interested in.

"She's the one who told me about it—just came out with it while we were talking, before she took off. But I don't remember exactly where she said she saw it."

Laafrit put his arm around Fifi again, and instead of fondling her tender forearm, he furtively pressed down hard on it as if he were trying to make her remember. Fifi didn't like it but she stopped herself from objecting. A look of fear appeared in her eyes as she remembered how Laafrit had interrogated her three years ago.

"If you can't remember," he said, "we'll have to go down to the station to talk it over in peace and quiet."

"I don't have anything more to tell you," she insisted, pleading with him.

Laafrit took a deep breath and looked around the place. No one was paying them any attention. He checked the scene again and went back to business.

"Sit back and calm down," he said. "I'll make it easy for you. Where'd your friend tell you about the gun?"

Fifi was smoking nervously as if she'd fallen into a trap.

"At La Lambada, I think. She was drunk. We ran into each other in the bathroom. I remember she stood in front of the mirror and pointed at it with her hands together like a gun, saying: 'Bang . . . bang . . . bang . . . !' She asked me if I'd ever touched a real gun. I said no, and she told me she had. She said it was heavy."

"Where was she when she saw it?" demanded Laafrit. He was trying to control his nerves.

"In Martil. It was last August, I think, but I don't know if she really saw a gun there or if she was just kidding around."

Laafrit felt he still hadn't gotten anything really useful from Fifi.

"Who was she staying with in Martil?"

"I didn't ask her," Fifi replied, coughing.

She took out a tissue and put it on the counter in front of her.

"There's this guy," she continued. "When I find him, he'll save us all this trouble."

Laafrit looked at her hopefully.

"Who?"

"His name's Fouad. Faouzia was madly in love with him. If you give me a little time, I'll find him and ask about it."

"He's the one she was with in Martil?"

"I don't know."

"What's his full name?"

"I don't know. She was always telling me about Fouad but I only saw him with her a couple times."

"Where?"

"Always at the same spot. Probably La Lambada."

"What about his address? The places he goes? His friends?"

She shook her head with a hint of regret.

"If you give me some time, I'll ask around for you. He goes out every night."

"Has Faouzia called you from Italy yet?"

"No."

Laafrit stopped a second to think.

"Who'll you ask?"

"I have my ways," she said, dodging his question.

"I want to know."

She put out her cigarette and twisted the tissue between her fingers.

"You want to know everything," she said, trying to hide the aggravation in her voice. "Fine. I've got my own informants, the guys who wander through all the Tangier bars and nightclubs selling food and cigarettes. When I want to know how things are in other places or where one of my customers is hiding from me, I pay these guys to find out. They know Faouzia and her lover Fouad, too. I'll have them look in all the bars and clubs. When they see him, they'll tell me and I'll let you know."

"But you're dancing at Scheherazade tonight," Laafrit countered, pleased with her idea.

"Don't worry. Trust me."

As if asking for sympathy, she squeezed his hand affectionately and indicated that she wanted to go. Laafrit hesitated, as if he was afraid he was letting her escape.

"I'll call you," she insisted.

"Wait," said Laafrit, grabbing her by the arm. "I don't want him to know the cops are behind it."

He looked down at his watch.

"If you don't find him," he added, "I'll have to take you downtown to give us a description of him. Call any time. You've got my cell number."

Fifi nodded and asked for her coat. She left quickly, as if she'd just made a stupid mistake.

Laafrit finished his drink in a single gulp. When Nadia appeared in front of him, he motioned with his hand to stop her from taking the glass but she ignored him and brought him a double.

"Want to get me drunk tonight?" Laafrit joked.

She leaned forward, her full breasts pressed together in front of him.

"If only I could . . ." she said, smiling sweetly.

Nadia put a cigarette between her lips and Laafrit lit it. She touched his hand gently and then slyly brought her glass over.

"You're not going to drink alone," she said. "Cheers!"

Laafrit was planning on taking off so he could have a chance to think but he looked at his glass and swayed a little. He convinced himself these rounds of whiskey would lighten his work, push him to think in more productive directions, and free his mind. He looked at Nadia's chest shamelessly, burped, and decided he had the right to take advantage of a little R and R since he wasn't on duty. What he was doing now was conducting investigations on his own initiative, unassigned. That wasn't anything to regret. He told himself that, if it hadn't been for his interest in the case, sitting here would have been cold and boring. For a while now, the only things that still excited him had been solving crimes and using others while he was working a case. If you're a cop for a day, that means you're a cop forever, everywhere you go. But, he told himself (not for the first time), as you use others, they're using you.

Nadia put out her cigarette, looked at her red fingernails, and swayed her head with the music, pulling Laafrit out of his distraction. At the sight of her flirtatious motions, Laafrit thought it'd be hard to get away from her to enjoy some time alone. He made up his mind to finish his drink and take off but Nadia suddenly livened up. She sang a saucy part of the song along with the music. This got on Laafrit's nerves. He thought it was just a veil and he felt Nadia was watching him. In fact, he was convinced she'd been watching him since he got there.

At this point, he decided to give her that calculating look he used to veil his true intentions. It was the look of a cop searching for clues. This was a useful deception: Nadia took a few steps back and came to a stop. The look nailed her down and made her anxious. She turned her eyes to the side. Laafrit let out a laugh and pointed at her with his index finger as if accusing her of something.

"Is there something you want to tell me?" he asked.

Suddenly, her face filled with an imploring look and confusion weighed heavily on her movements. She blushed.

"I got divorced, sir, five years ago, as soon as I got pregnant," she said to him, her eyes on the ground. "My son Karim's now four and my ex-husband lives in Tetouan, working as a smuggler. He makes a ton of money and wastes it all on whores in nightclubs. I put my son Karim in the most expensive school because I want him to get the best education from early on. But it's very expensive and his father hasn't given him even a carton of milk since the divorce. On my own, sir, I support a family of seven. My father's old and my mother's sick with kidney failure. I have five brothers. One's a teacher but the rest are unemployed.

"My ex plays with his money. Since the day we got divorced, he hasn't given me a penny of support. The courts say: 'Give us his address and we'll go arrest him.' But all I know is he's in Tetouan. Sir, you must have friends there . . ."

Laafrit signaled he'd heard enough. He took out his small notebook.

"What's his name?" he asked, refusing to hear any more pleading.

"Mohamed Benhammad, sir."

"You sure he's in Tetouan?" added the detective, taking down the name.

Nadia's voice rattled as she indicated yes. Tears took her by surprise, so she hid her face in her palms and hurried into the back room. Only then did Laafrit notice the lit cigarette between his fingers. He took a long drag and put it out in the ashtray.

The detective's mood was ruined, so he gulped down what was left in his glass and got ready to go. A customer walked up to the bar next to Laafrit and hit his hand on the counter, calling out for Nadia. She returned from the back room, moving to the music, repeating the same saucy lines like nothing had happened. She didn't even look in Laafrit's direction. It seemed she'd dropped her veil—it had done its job.

5

IT WAS TWO THIRTY IN the morning when the cell phone next to his pillow rang. Laafrit had been asleep for only two hours. He got home a bit before midnight and spent about fifteen minutes coming on to his wife, who fended off his advances because she refused to have sex with him when his breath reeked of wine. Laafrit didn't insist and turned to the other side where Reem was sleeping in her toddler bed.

Laafrit tried to organize his thoughts about the case, doing his best not to overlook anything. He rejected the Sebta hypothesis because it would have been impossible for the bodies to stay so close to each other over such a long distance that they washed up in the same general area.

He found himself thinking about Fifi, putting her at the center of things. He knew she'd bought her family a luxurious apartment in the heart of Tangier and that she lived under the watchful eye of her mother, who'd once been a prostitute. After Fifi's father died, the only thing he left Fifi's mother were four children to take care of. As sleep played with his eyes, Laafrit remembered the day he had interrogated Fifi and her mother. With all that whiskey in him, he couldn't dismiss Nadia, who entered the picture too. When the phone rang, the three women were moving back and forth in Laafrit's dream.

Naeema had to prod Laafrit several times to get him to pick up the phone. She was afraid the ringing would wake up Reem.

"Hello," he answered quickly, waking up.

"It's Fifi," she said, letting out a loud laugh in his ear. "You sleeping?"

He forced himself to open his eyes and lifted his head off the pillow.

"No," he said, fighting back a yawn. "I was waiting for you to call."

"Listen, your man's at the Cave."

Laafrit pushed back the blankets and stood up.

"Leave the room or you'll wake the girl," his wife whispered, chiding him.

Laafrit felt the coldness of the ground as he made his way in the dark with the phone pressed to his ear.

"You said the Cave, but how'll I recognize him?"

"You can't miss him," Fifi said, sounding a bit drunk. "He's got a baseball cap on. They call him 'the guy who's got no problem with his hair.'"

"He has long hair?" asked Laafrit.

"It goes past his shoulders. He wears it in a ponytail."

Laafrit couldn't stop himself from asking the obvious question: "Who gave you the information?"

"Limpy, a street peddler. He charged me fifty dirhams for it."

Laafrit immediately got off the phone with her. As he was calling the station, he heard a woman outside yelling for help, as well as a man who sounded as if he was barking. He finished dialing.

"Hello, who's this?" asked the detective.

"Who's this? Laafrit?" a thick, sleepy voice responded.

"Inspector Lamalki?"

"Yes," the inspector said, coming to life.

"Send two squad cars together with backup to the Cave nightclub. Lock the doors and don't let anyone out until I get there. Understood?"

"Affirmative."

Laafrit went out to the balcony overlooking the narrow street to see where all the yelling was coming from. The street was empty and all the houses were dark except for the last one. He then remembered the teacher.

"That woman deserves protection," he told himself.

The club was in the center of town, near the train station and on a street that had a big sign for tourists and lovers of outdoor cafés under the shadow of tall palm trees. There was a grassy passageway leading up to the street and ending in an open-air café. It continued on to the port, the train station, the beach, and finally to the sea opening onto the Iberian borders.

The Cave was crammed between travel agencies marked by bright outdoor signs and neon lights left on inside. Laafrit found the street blocked off, with cop cars forming barriers to prevent bystanders from getting too close. This street never slept, and most of the cafés here stayed open until dawn, as did the surrounding bocadillo joints and hole-in-the-wall restaurants, sausage-cart vendors, and guys exchanging money and selling smuggled cigarettes and hash. Add to that mix the locals, most of them vagabonds, glue sniffers, and the destitute.

Laafrit used his high beams to clear the road. He pulled up directly in front of the club, where there were two uniformed cops standing guard. Behind them a bunch of women crowded around the peephole of the club's iron gate, haggling with the cops and trying to get in.

"A hundred dirhams to let us in!" said one.

"Two hundred!" said another.

"Three hundred and a kiss!" yelled a third.

The two young cops stopped laughing when they saw the detective's car pull up.

Laafrit met them and wondered if he should drag everyone inside to the station, take just a few, or make a beeline for his man. He ordered the front door opened and asked the two bouncers, who looked like retired weightlifting champions, to come outside. The detective gave them a description of Fouad and mentioned Faouzia, who had emigrated to Italy on a fake passport. Laafrit asked them for more information, and the larger of the two said they should avoid causing any panic inside. They didn't want the women to get hysterical, especially since it'd hurt business for the next few days. He suggested bringing Fouad out raised up in the air like a butterfly.

After the two bouncers carried Fouad out, Laafrit told them to put him down on the ground. He was so drunk he couldn't stand up on his own. Fouad wasn't older than thirty. He was wearing a jacket and had a gold chain without a pendant around his neck. He also had on a cap with the words "World Golf Club." As soon as the detective pulled off the cap, he was struck by the man's feminine beauty, especially when he saw Fouad's soft fine hair dangling down, covering his drowsy eyes.

The detective exchanged glances with the bouncers, who immediately knew what Laafrit had in mind. The two quickly tossed Fouad into the back of the police van, where he collapsed in a heap, as if this was what he had been longing to do.

At the station, Laafrit couldn't wake Fouad up, despite a few light slaps and tugs on his hair. He went through Fouad's pockets and found a small sheet of hash wrapped in tinfoil, a box of Marlboros, a wad of more than a thousand dirhams, his ID, and a photo of a beautiful girl about twenty years old who had to be Faouzia. When Laafrit patted down Fouad's legs, he found a knife in a leather sheath tucked into one of his socks. Laafrit gave the ID to the inspector, who was busy at the computer, and told him to keep Fouad in the holding cell until morning.

Laafrit had breakfast in the café opposite the station. It was seven thirty. He put the first menthol lozenge of the day in his mouth and tried to guess what would happen with Fouad.

Before he could collect his thoughts, however, Inspector Lamalki came into the café, his eyes bloodshot from being up all night. Lamalki had just finished the graveyard shift and was surprised to see Laafrit. He asked for a café au lait and a cheese croissant.

"You've been waiting for this guy," said Lamalki. "What'd you want out of him?"

"Does he have any priors?" asked Laafrit.

"A year in jail for smuggling and resisting arrest."

"The bouncer at the Cave told me he's a second-rate cigarette smuggler."

"He's pretty like a woman," the inspector said, smiling. "God protect him. There's a guy in his cell who's a real pervert."

Laafrit immediately stood up with an alarmed look. He remembered the last time they brought someone in passed out drunk and threw him in the holding cell for the night. The next morning, they found him dead. The detective on duty that day was put under investigation. The DA said standard procedures weren't followed. In that situation, they should have taken the drunk to the hospital first, not to jail.

Laafrit rushed to the station, imagining the disaster that'd happen to him if he found Fouad dead, or worse.

When the detective got to the holding area, he found Fouad squatting with his head between his knees. The other guy in the cell was fast asleep and didn't stop snoring, despite all the noise when Laafrit unlocked the iron gate and swung it open. Laafrit walked into the cell and grabbed his man by the arm.

"Good morning," he said sarcastically. "Sleep well?"

Fouad didn't answer. His face was creased and his eyes were blood red. Fouad limped out of the cell slowly, as if he had a problem with his foot. Laafrit walked ahead of him in the corridor. The detective opened his office door and pushed him inside. Fouad staggered and reeled, almost colliding with the metal filing cabinet. Laafrit slapped the desk and told him to sit down with a threatening look.

"I don't have time to waste on you," he said as if he were getting ready to break his neck. "I want to know where the gun is."

Fouad pursed his lips as if he just heard a joke.

"Why am I here? What'd I do?" he asked in a rough voice, after a moment of silence.

Laafrit stared at him briefly and realized Fouad really didn't get what was going on. The detective took off his jacket and put it on the hook. He rolled up his sleeves slowly and then waved his fist in front of Fouad's face.

"I asked you, where's the gun?"

Fouad laughed as if he'd heard a joke, but the detective immediately slapped him across the face. Fouad fell out of his seat, without making a sound. Laafrit pulled him up by his long hair and put him back on the chair.

"Awake now?"

Laafrit then moved behind him, making Fouad think the next blow could come at any moment.

"I don't have a gun!" Fouad yelled out, choked with tears and shaking his head.

Laafrit stroked Fouad's silky hair with feigned tenderness and then sat on the edge of the desk in front of him. He looked at Fouad for a while until the silence in the office became heavy and unnerving. The detective stood up again, opened a drawer, and took out the picture of the girl he'd found on Fouad.

"Who's this?"

"A friend of mine."

"What's her name?"

"Faouzia."

"Her family name?"

"Bint el-Hussein."

"Where does she live?"

"She used to live on Place Taureaux."

"Where's she now?"

"She emigrated to Italy."

"When?"

"Two, three months ago."

"Before she left, you spent August with her in Martil, right?"

Fouad trembled as he felt his swollen cheek.

"I didn't spend a month with her in Martil," he said in a firm voice. "I visited her only once."

Laafrit leaned toward Fouad.

"You visited her once? Who was she with then?"

Fouad's hesitation made Laafrit think he was lying. The detective grabbed him by the neck and pressed down hard.

"Who was she with in Martil?"

Laafrit let go. Fouad swallowed with difficulty, gasping for air.

"With . . . with a boyfriend of hers."

"And who are you? Her pimp?" yelled Laafrit as a terrifying look flashed in his eyes.

"I'm not her only boyfriend!" he said.

Laafrit was convinced Fouad was feeding him half-truths. The detective lifted his arm menacingly, getting ready to slap him again. When he saw fear fill Fouad's eyes, he hit the metal filing cabinet, which made a terrifying noise and mixed with Laafrit's shouting.

"Faouzia confessed to our men in Italy she saw a gun on you!" yelled Laafrit.

Fouad was obviously confused, as if the reason for the interrogation wasn't what he had anticipated. Laafrit noticed this but didn't want to shift gears. He was sure Fouad was hiding a lot of things, but what interested Laafrit was the gun. The detective gave him a second to collect himself.

"Faouzia told you I have a gun?" Fouad asked, startled.

"She confessed she spent the summer vacation with you in Martil," said Laafrit, lightening his aggressive tone. "And that she saw a gun on you."

"And where'd she spend the vacation with me in Martil?" said Fouad, laughing, as if he was making fun of himself. "I don't have a tent there, let alone an apartment."

Laafrit sat down and relaxed in his chair. He put a lozenge in his mouth and glared at Fouad provocatively.

"Go ahead, tell me your lies," he said, the lozenge lightening the sharpness of his voice. "I'll do everything in my power to put up with them and hear you out."

Fouad's fear began to recede. He was bent on making sure he didn't mix up his facts. He didn't want to implicate himself by accidentally confessing to something totally unrelated.

"If you want information about a gun," he said in a confident voice, "I once saw one at Issa Karami's place."

When Laafrit heard this, he tried to hide his excitement. He acted as if he didn't trust a word Fouad told him.

"Go on, go on," he said, shaking his head disinterestedly.

Fouad didn't hold back. He spoke spontaneously as if purging himself of secrets that didn't have anything to do with him.

"Faouzia didn't tell you anything. She called me two days ago from Italy. I've been with her for more than three years. The girl's in love with me but that didn't stop her from leaving without me. I didn't care since I'm not going to marry her. To be honest, she's a prostitute but she's not professional or anything like that. She doesn't go with any old bum off the street. She's got her preferred customers and Issa Karami's one of them. He's a big-time drug dealer in Spain and even has a Spanish passport. When Issa comes to town, Faouzia abandons me and everyone else and takes up with him until he takes off.

"The important thing is that Issa has an apartment in Martil, where he always spends August, together with Faouzia. But she used to miss me so much, she'd called me whenever she got the chance. Last August, she asked me to come to Martil. She told me she'd be alone. We met at the Garden Bar at eight. I found her there sitting alone, with a beer and a pack of Marlboros in front of her. When I tried to sit down, she got angry and told me to take a hike, acting like she didn't even know me. I ignored her and sat down, but she said without looking at me that the waiter was watching her. Issa got a call for a quick trip to Tangier and he told her to wait for him at the bar until it closed. If he came back, great. If not, the waiter would take her home. She told me I had to wait around but not to get too close. If I saw Issa, I had to beat it. If he didn't make it, I was supposed to follow her when the waiter took her home.

"So that's what happened. I sat far away and drank some beers. Issa didn't show up, so after midnight I did what she told me. I left the bar and waited around outside so no one would see me. After a while, Faouzia left with the waiter and I followed them back to Issa's.

"You know Martil. The Paseo is packed till morning. The important thing's that I followed them to a building opposite the Corniche. There the waiter said goodbye to Faouzia and took off. She went upstairs, and five minutes later she looked for me from the balcony and signaled that I should come up.

"I won't lie to you. I was so scared I almost died. When I got to the apartment, the door was unlocked. I pushed it open and went in. Faouzia ran over to lock it, and then hugged me. She was missing me and said she couldn't wait any more. She calmed me down about Issa, saying he wouldn't be back. I was still scared to death. I wandered around the apartment. It was on the second floor. I was thinking if Issa came back all of a sudden, I'd jump out the kitchen window.

"Anyway, we had some drinks. You know, we spent the night talking about everything. Faouzia told me Issa went to Tangier to meet some friends coming in from Ireland. Then she got up, opened the closet, and took out his Spanish passport. We flipped through it and looked at the stamps from the countries he's visited. I got tired and started falling asleep but Faouzia said I had to stay up till morning.

"Some time passed and I thought she was in the bathroom, but she came out of the bedroom holding a gun. She pointed it at me and said: 'Put 'em up!' like in the movies. I didn't pay her any attention, since I thought the gun was fake. It looked like a kid's toy. But she told me it was real. And loaded. When she put it in my hands, I knew she wasn't kidding. It was really heavy. I don't have to tell you I was dying I was so scared. If God decided that Issa would come back and find me in his house like that, he'd have killed me with that gun in a second.

"I told Faouzia to put it back where she found it but there she was, acting like a big shot, standing in front of the mirror and making sounds like she was shooting it. She was drunk and I had a headache so I took off before dawn."

Laafrit kept silent, looking at Fouad carefully. Fouad seemed less afraid than before and he was ready to keep talking.

"That's a tidy little story," Laafrit said without shifting in his seat. "We'll check it out, piece by piece. And if I find out you've wasted my time here with lies . . ."

Fouad looked a bit more relaxed. He took his cap out of his pocket and put it on.

"So, where does Issa Karami live?" asked the detective.

"Can you give me a cigarette?" asked Fouad timidly.

Laafrit opened the drawer and took out Fouad's pack of cigarettes, the piece of hash, and the knife.

"There was more than a thousand dirhams in my pocket yesterday," protested Fouad.

Laafrit took the money out of the drawer, showed it to Fouad, and put it back.

"This is evidence against you," he said, pointing to the hash and the knife.

Fouad lit a cigarette and took a series of quick drags.

"Issa Karami lives in Spain," he said, looking at his cigarette. "And he has the apartment I told you about in Martil. From what Faouzia told me, he's from El Jebha."

"Doesn't he have a place here in Tangier?"

"I don't know. When he's in town, he stays with Faouzia at a hotel."

"Is Issa in Morocco now?"

"I don't know. He usually doesn't come back this time of year."

Laafrit didn't want to dig any deeper into Fouad's life. The detective had a clear enough picture of him. Fouad was just a two-bit smuggler and part-time pimp. From the looks of him, Laafrit thought he might even be queer.

The next step wasn't clear to Laafrit. He was afraid of messing around and wasting time. But what was giving him some satisfaction was that he'd get hold of that gun soon. As long as he decided to believe Fouad, despite having no real reason to, he had to focus before rushing on to anything else. And what he wanted was to make his way step by step to the gun. Because of that, he knew he had to trace exactly how it got into the country and past the inspection and control points. All the smugglers, dealers, and crooks knew what it meant to smuggle a gun into Morocco.

He paced around his office, feeling satisfied with his progress. If the gun had fulfilled its function of killing the still-unidentified victim, it must still be around somewhere, since the killer wouldn't have just gotten rid of it by tossing it into the sea or dropping it down some sewer drain. That's something that happens in Europe, where guns are sold the way they sell tins of sardines here. But if it really was Issa Karami who had managed to get the gun into the country, he wouldn't be stupid enough to try to risk getting it out. Any fool knew how dangerous that'd be.

Looking out the window toward the port, Laafrit followed a boat that appeared in the middle of the sea like a magnificent white bird. He suddenly turned toward Fouad.

"Do you remember where Issa Karami's apartment is in Martil?"

"It's in a three-story building on the Corniche," said Fouad without the least hesitation.

6

THE FIAT REACHED TETOUAN, ABOUT ten kilometers from Martil, in less than an hour. Fouad sat in the back next to Inspector Abdellah, the forensics agent, while Laafrit sat in the front next to Inspector Allal, who was at the wheel. At first they talked about the case, but Laafrit was tired from the night before and wanted to take advantage of the drive to doze.

Abdellah coughed a number of times, as if he were hesitating before doing something. Then he started humming, pretending that he was trying to hum just to himself, but the refrain "there is no God but God" filled his voice with such religious fervor it soon slipped through his lips audibly. But really, he was testing if Laafrit was in as deep a sleep as he appeared to be. Allal too started repeating the refrain, but the burning thirst reached its limit with Abdellah. He couldn't restrain himself and gave free rein to his voice:

The glance became clear, hadra became sublime,
    The good news came to the people of God.
Those intoxicated by good tidings arose
    And made a great party, thanks be to God.

The words mixed pleasingly in Laafrit's head. What surprised him most was Abdellah's touching voice, full of vibrato. He was reciting with an inner strength, savoring the words and pronouncing them loaded with emotion, revealing their essence as if he was bringing to them the vastness of life. His face was radiant with joy and when he turned to Fouad, who was sitting next to him, he urged him to repeat the refrain. That's how the police car came into Tetouan, shaking with praises of the Prophet until it stopped in front of the main police station.

In Tetouan, the case took a different direction. When Laafrit entered the station, he found the commissioner waiting for him. Despite his high rank, the commissioner pulled his tall frame out of his chair, greeted Laafrit, and told him he had requested permission from the DA to search the suspect's apartment. He also said he had given instructions to the Martil police to offer assistance. The commissioner suggested he accompany them to Issa's apartment, but Laafrit convinced him it was only a routine search as part of an investigation that was still in the initial stages.

Before they took off for Martil, Laafrit spoke alone with Inspector Firqash, who he'd known for years. He gave him the name of Mohamed Benhammad—Nadia's ex-husband, the deadbeat dad—and asked the inspector to arrest him and transfer him to Tangier.

Martil was a small coastal city and most of its buildings were empty during the off-season, since the majority of them were owned by Moroccans working abroad. There was only one police station with ten men at the most and a single police van that needed repairs and probably didn't even run.

When the Fiat reached the station and the cops exchanged greetings, Laafrit asked the Martil detective about Issa Karami. He didn't have the slightest idea who he was. The cops then all went together down to the Corniche. When they arrived at the start of the road, Fouad asked them to pull over so he could look for the building. Before they got out of the car, Abdellah took out his handcuffs and, in a voice that had no connection whatsoever to his gentle chanting on the way to Tetouan, told Fouad to spread his hands.

From the description Fouad had given him, Laafrit recognized the building even before Fouad pointed it out. It had three stories with wide balconies overlooking the sea. Only a neglected sand-covered road separated it from the shore. The area was deserted except for a grocer and a small storefront full of phone booths. Surprised to see a crowd of cops, the two storeowners came out and stood in their doorways.

"Call them over as witnesses for the search," Laafrit told the Martil detective, eyeing the two men.

Like the nearby buildings, this one was unoccupied. Sand lay on the stairs. There were double doors: a beautiful inner wooden door matching the modern facade of the building, and another door added to the outside. It was like a gate for a cage of ferocious animals: iron bars intersected with thick locks.

"The residents only come here in the summer," one of the Martil cops said, explaining the thick locks. "Otherwise the buildings are empty, and people worry about their things."

They took turns examining the locks. Laafrit thought they'd have to bring a welder and a carpenter to get through the front door. Leaving the group, he circled the building. Behind it was an abandoned square, which the building's back windows overlooked. It seemed to Laafrit breaking a window would be easier than getting through the front door.

They asked some construction workers at a nearby site for help, and in less than half an hour, Laafrit was leading the way up the stairs. He jumped into the kitchen and Allal, Abdellah, and Fouad, without the handcuffs, soon followed. The Martil cop and the two witnesses came in last.

Laafrit was surprised when he flipped the light switch and the place lit up. The Martil cop understood Laafrit's confusion.

"The owner must've given his bank number to the electric company so they deduct the bill directly from his account," the cop explained.

Laafrit had trouble opening the kitchen door. He had to push hard until he finally got the latch open. When he turned on the rest of the lights, he saw the living room was decked out in the latest trends: fancy antiques, expensive wooden cupboards filled with china and crystal, and couches draped in white covers. Gold-framed pictures adorned the walls.

The apartment was spacious. It had four bedrooms and Laafrit noticed while looking around that the whole place was furnished luxuriously, almost entirely with foreign things. His general impression was that nothing was out of place. He decided it was pointless to look for the gun anywhere else besides the bedroom.

In the bedroom, Laafrit opened the wardrobe and found it full of summer clothes: button-down shorts, T-shirts, towels, sports shoes, and hats. There were also boxes full of gifts. Laafrit figured Issa must have forgotten to give them out. There wasn't much else in the room worth searching through, just a big bed, a dressing mirror, and two small bedside tables, each with a lamp on top.

Should he start looking inside everything? Laafrit usually left the places he searched clean, and he didn't want the others getting involved. He had a plan in his head. If Issa hadn't taken any precautions with Faouzia and he left the gun out so she could play with it, that meant he was acting as if it was no big deal to have a gun in the house.

After searching the drawers, Laafrit went back to the wardrobe and began looking through the clothes. All of a sudden the gun appeared, like a timid mouse. Laafrit looked over at the others and smiled. He took a white tissue out of his pocket, lifted the revolver by its barrel, and looked at it closely. Abdellah rushed over, surprised.

"We got it, Laafrit," he said in rapturous tones, gripping it. "Beretta nine-millimeter, same as the murder weapon."

*

Back in Tangier, there was a huge uproar in the commissioner's office. Laafrit got so many pats on his shoulder that his jacket hung down loosely. Everyone congratulated him with firm handshakes. Trying not to sound self-serving, Laafrit gave the commissioner a report on the steps he took to recover the gun. The commissioner let out a boisterous laugh and then lifted up a fax.

"We got this right after you left for Martil," he said exuberantly. "They identified one of the victims at Central. His name's Driss el-Yamani, from Beni Mellal. We contacted the police down there and the victim's brother's on his way here to ID the body."

Laafrit sat up in his chair.

"Which one is he?"

"Number three. One of the drowned men, not the shooting victim."

Laafrit looked closely at the picture of el-Yamani's body the commissioner handed him.

"And Issa Karami?" the detective asked.

"We gave his name to Central and the border police. We're still waiting on word from them."

Laafrit stole a glance at his watch. It was a bit after three o'clock. He yawned and stretched his arms.

"Commissioner, I wanted to let you know that I have not eaten lunch yet," the detective said in an official tone. "And I only slept a little last night."

The commissioner saw the obvious exhaustion on Laafrit's face.

"Go home immediately and don't come back until tomorrow morning," he said, as if giving a direct order.

Just as Laafrit was about to leave the station, he heard the clicking of high heels, and all of a sudden he saw his neighbor, the teacher, coming from the end of the corridor with her husband dawdling behind her.

"Shit! Shit!" Laafrit repeated to himself, wanting to escape. He had completely forgotten about his three o'clock appointment.

7

AT TEN O'CLOCK THE NEXT morning, the cop at the reception desk led a young man to Laafrit's office. The detective immediately knew it was the brother of victim number three.

Laafrit greeted him warmly and asked him to sit down. After a few pleasantries, the detective asked him for his ID and then put a photo of drowning victim number three in front of him. Laafrit watched the kid's expression closely as he stared at the picture in disbelief. The kid began scrutinizing the picture, holding it with his thumb. His feelings were a mixture of confusion and grief.

"Tell me, Abdel-Jalil, do you recognize the man in the photo?" asked Laafrit.

The kid shook his head without looking up from the photo. He stayed silent.

"You'll be more sure when you see him at the morgue," said Laafrit. "What's your brother's name?"

"Driss."

Laafrit noticed Abdel-Jalil was trembling in a way that indicated real grief. He was more than twenty years old but he had a bunch of pimples scattered across his face and his appearance indicated he was dirt poor.

It seemed he was trying hard to open his mouth and that he was exasperated by the thoughts that were surfacing. Appreciating the delicate situation, Laafrit kept in check the urge to get some information out of the kid. He got up to leave so Abdel-Jalil could have a chance to calm down.

"What happened to my brother?" Abdel-Jalil asked suddenly in an upset voice.

"He washed ashore here in Tangier," Laafrit said, filling his voice with grief. "No doubt he told you he was going to hrig?"

Abdel-Jalil lifted the picture and looked at it again in disbelief.

"But," he said, confused, "my brother hrigged two years ago. He got to Spain safely with a group of guys from our neighborhood. They all live in Almería. He calls us all the time."

Laafrit was bewildered, and the papers got mixed up in front of him.

"When's the last time he called you?" asked the detective, unable to control his surprise.

"A week ago. I'm the one who talked to him. He said everything was great."

Laafrit smiled doubtfully and put an end to the conversation. There had to be a mistake.

"Look, there might be some misunderstanding," he said, getting up quickly. "We'll talk after you see the body."

When they got to the morgue, Laafrit evaded the medical examiner's questions. He didn't want to talk until Abdel-Jalil had positively identified his brother's body. The professor responded immediately. He pulled opened the four freezer drawers nervously and left the observation room with his silent shuffling steps. The coroner's strange mannerisms only increased Abdel-Jalil's anxiety. Abdel-Jalil shut his eyes for a long time, unable to get close to the bodies.

"Go on," said Laafrit. "Do everything you can to get a grip on yourself."

Abdel-Jalil stayed about half a meter from the bodies. He put his hand over his mouth, unable to stop trembling. He looked at the first corpse and his eyes widened. All of a sudden, he overcame his fear and surged forward to look closely at the four bodies. A strange expression appeared on his face and the shock produced a sharp reaction that rippled through his body. His heart beat furiously and the blood drained from his face. Slapping himself on the cheek a number of times, he staggered backward. Laafrit rushed over to Abdel-Jalil and propped him up, telling him he had to calm down. But the kid started screaming and flailing as if he wanted to hit his head against the wall.

Professor Abdel-Majid came back quickly with a group of assistants. When he saw the hysteria that had seized the kid, he rushed to get the corpses back in the freezer.

"These things happen," he said to Laafrit. "A lot of people can't bear to see the dead."

"They're all from my neighborhood!" Abdel-Jalil said in a cracking voice.

"Did you see your brother?" asked Laafrit.

The shock had clearly taken its toll on Abdel-Jalil and he looked like he was on the verge of passing out. Laafrit moved away from him and left him with the assistants. He thought for the first time that this kid, in addition to the state of shock, was suffering from stress and insomnia since he had no doubt spent the entire night on the bus and then the train, making his way to Tangier from Beni Mellal, which was about six hundred kilometers south. Maybe Abdel-Jalil hadn't slept a wink. Maybe he hadn't had breakfast yet either.

When they left the morgue, Laafrit tried to get the kid's mind off the tragedy. He asked about the trip and how the police at Beni Mellal broke the news to his family. Abdel-Jalil only responded with mumbles, as if he had tried but failed to extract the words from his lips.

Laafrit parked the Fiat opposite the police station and instead of just taking the kid inside, he walked him over to the café next door and told him gently to have some breakfast. Despite the detective's insistence, Abdel-Jalil didn't take more than two sips of his tea and he didn't touch the raghif he ordered or anything else Laafrit offered him. For his part, the detective was impatient to know exactly what had happened to Abdel-Jalil's brother.

When they got back to the station, Abdel-Jalil asked Laafrit if he could smoke. The detective put an ashtray in front of him.

"So," said Laafrit, doing everything he could to deal with him gently, "you recognized the four bodies. You said they're all from your neighborhood?"

Laafrit paused. Abdel-Jalil wasn't looking at what was in front of him. He stared off into space as if recalling a distant memory. Laafrit gave the kid a moment to collect himself and then put the question to him another way.

"Can you tell me the names of the others?"

"Mohamed Bensallam, Jamal el-Kaidi, and Hicham el-Ouni," he muttered, still in a state of shock.

"In addition to your brother, Driss el-Yamani?" asked Laafrit. "You said in the morgue they were all from your neighborhood?"

"Yeah, except for Bensallam's family. They moved to Hayy el-Falah two months ago."

"Do the families have any idea what happened to them?"

"No."

"You sure the bodies you saw in the morgue are them? If you have any doubt, we can go back."

Abdel-Jalil only took two drags from his cigarette. He put it on the edge of the ashtray and let it sit there burning.

"I'm pressing," said Laafrit, "because we'll have to call their families and ask them to come identify the bodies, just as you did."

Abdel-Jalil nodded.

"Good," said Laafrit. "You said your brother hrigged two years ago."

"Yeah, with Jamal el-Kaidi, Hicham el-Ouni, and Jaouad Benmousa."

Laafrit took out headshots of the victims and put them side by side in front of Abdel-Jalil. The detective asked him to name each one separately so he could write it on the back of each photo. When he got to the picture of the shooting victim, Abdel-Jalil hesitated.

"But Mohamed Bensallam was in Beni Mellal this summer," he said, confused. "He came back in a big expensive car, bought a house, got married, and had a huge wedding."

Laafrit found it hard to take in what he had just heard.

"How could a harrag come back to the country just like that?" asked Laafrit, as if doubting Abdel-Jalil. "Did he get legal papers?"

"Mohamed Bensallam," said Abdel-Majid, "was the first to hrig. That was five years ago. He lived in Almería and worked on a huge farm. Because he was good at what he did, the farm owner got him papers."

"When'd your brother and the others hrig?"

"Two years ago. The summer before last."

"The three of them hrigged at the same time?"

"There were four, but Jaouad Benmousa isn't here with the others."

"They all got there safely?"

"Yeah."

Laafrit looked grave.

"If I've got you right," he said, as if reining in his thoughts, "Mohamed Bensallam hrigged five years ago, lived in Almería, and managed to get papers. As for the others," he went on, turning over the photos so he could read their names, "Jamal el-Kaidi, Hicham el-Ouni, and your brother, Driss el-Yamani, they hrigged two years ago, got to Spain safely, and worked in Almería with Mohamed Bensallam. They're the four you identified at the morgue."

"But Jaouad Benmousa wasn't there with them," Abdel-Jalil said, letting out a moan.

Laafrit shook his head, trying to understand what was going on. He realized that the case, instead of clearing up, was only becoming more confusing.

81

8

THE REST OF THE VICTIMS' families arrived from Beni Mellal at six in the morning the next day and waited at the station's main entrance, weeping loudly. When Laafrit got there at eight thirty, the mourning had died down somewhat. There was no reason for Laafrit to accompany the family to the morgue, so he had Inspectors Allal and Abdellah go with them and question them. Laafrit asked the father of the shooting victim, Lakbir Bensallam, to stay with him at the station. The old man was clearly blind. When Bensallam's father protested, Laafrit tried to convince him as best he could.

"You can't even see, uncle," said Laafrit. "You won't be able to help in the identification. It's enough for your wife to go."

Laafrit helped him sit down, almost forcing the old man not to go.

Si Lakbir was more than seventy years old. His face was covered with wrinkles and his eyes were hidden behind thick black glasses. He was wearing two djellabas, one on top of the other, and his head was wrapped in an embroidered turban he straightened every now and then, even though it wasn't out of place.

Laafrit couldn't get him to open up about his son. The detective was afraid the old man would be too grief stricken. He definitely hadn't been expecting such a painful blow. The old man was clearly still holding out hope the whole thing would turn out to be a big mistake. His hope was transferred to the detective, so, as a kind of precaution, Laafrit bided his time until the phone rang. He picked up the receiver and it was Inspector Allal calling from the morgue. Laafrit insisted on speaking in French so the old man wouldn't understand. The inspector confirmed what Abdel-Jalil had said the day before—the bodies were now all positively identified. After hanging up, Laafrit turned to the old man, who was sitting opposite him, and told him that his wife had identified the body of their son.

"Allahu Akbar, Allahu Akbar, Allahu Akbar!" repeated the old man, raising his head and index finger to the office ceiling.

He made a fist and tucked it into his djellaba pocket. He then raised it up and began rubbing his chest as if to help him digest the disaster. Laafrit thought the old man was trying to express his acceptance of God's will. But the shock was so powerful that the old man took off his glasses to wipe away his tears. Laafrit moved back. The old man's eyes were shut completely, but teardrops nonetheless slid down as if they were leaking from above his eyelids.

"I haven't cried in thirty years," he said with an odd smile. *"There is no power and no strength save in God."*

"May God give you patience, uncle," said Laafrit delicately. "If you want to postpone our talk, I don't have any objections."

The old man put his glasses back on and tried in vain to get a grip on his grief. He gritted his teeth and waved his hand as if he was going through memories of his son.

"Why are they killing our children?" he asked in a threatening tone, leaning over the desk. "The godless infidels!"

Laafrit was shocked.

"Who told you they were killed?"

"That's what the police in Beni Mellal told us. It's what everyone says. They're racists there. They kill immigrants like they kill flies. May God curse poverty."

Laafrit sat up straight.

"Please, uncle, when did your son hrig?"

"Five years ago. I sold the land I owned to help him pay the smugglers."

"I know he managed to get papers," said Laafrit, baiting the old man.

"May God be pleased with him," he said tenderly. "He was a real man, the only one from Beni Mellal who hrigged that managed to get papers."

"When did he get them?"

"More than two years ago. After he got them, he came home safe and sound. If I knew they were going to kill him, I wouldn't have let him go back. But it's God's will," he said in resignation.

"When did he go back to Beni Mellal the second time?"

"After he got his papers, he came back to Morocco four times. Last summer he bought a house, got married, and had a wedding party the whole town still talks about. But it's God's will, God's will."

"Was this the last time he came back?"

"No. He came home last November but he only stayed for a week."

"Uncle," said Laafrit, trying to hide his suspicions, "your son was coming back to Morocco a lot. Why?"

"He lived in Almería, my son. Like he told us, this Almería is not very far from our country. He'd leave in the morning and be home with us in Beni Mellal by nighttime."

"That's true, uncle," said Laafrit. "Did he usually drive back to Beni Mellal?"

"He came back by car the first time, when he got married, bought the house, and had a big wedding. God . . . God . . . His joy wasn't completed. It's God's fate."

"When he came back to Beni Mellal last time in November, was there any specific reason? It seems to me, uncle, that after a summer vacation, he stayed at work for less than two months before coming back."

"That last time, my son, he stayed with us for one day and then went to the Doukkala region."

"Why did he go to Doukkala?"

"He didn't tell us, my son."

"Where in Doukkala did he go?"

"I swear, my son, we didn't ask him. He said he was going to Doukkala and he left. When he came back, he stayed with us for another day and then went back to his work in Spain."

"He didn't tell you which town he went to?"

"No."

"Do you have family in the region?"

"No, my son."

"Does he have friends there?"

"Maybe, but only God knows."

"Did he go alone? With his wife or someone else?"

"He went alone."

"Didn't he tell his wife why he was going to Doukkala?"

"No. He said he had work there and left."

"Who'd he visit when he came back to Beni Mellal?"

"The family. He loved his family and never forgot any of us. He'd always bring gifts for everyone, kids and adults."

"And his friends?"

"He never forgot them either."

"Does he have friends outside Beni Mellal?"

"Only God knows, my son," the old man said, taking a deep breath. "But why all these questions?"

Laafrit was embarrassed. He felt he had pushed more than he should have, and paused before answering.

"Uncle, there's something regrettable I have to tell you. When your son washed ashore, he'd been shot four times. The other three drowned."

The man trembled and his turban slid to the side. He hit it with his hand to put it back into place. His lips moved, but he didn't utter a word.

"We don't believe your son was killed by racists," said Laafrit.

The man hit the edge of the desk and half rose.

"Who killed him?"

"We have the name of a suspect. Issa Karami. Have you heard that name before?"

"No, never," the old man replied without hesitating. "What's his connection to my son?"

"For now, only God knows. Issa Karami has an apartment in Martil and we found the gun there, the same one used to kill your son."

"Have you arrested him?" asked the old man impatiently.

"Soon, God willing, he'll be in our hands."

"Who's this man? How does he know my son?"

"Try to calm down, uncle," said Laafrit, his mood worsening.

He snuck a lozenge out of his pocket and put it under his tongue.

"What kind of work did your son do in Almería?"

"Farm work. My son's very good at it."

"Do you know the name of his employer?"

"Carlos . . . Gomez."

"Do you know who your son lived with in Almería?"

"The owner gave him a place to stay on his farm. My son really liked him. He was always saying good things about him and he'd bring him gifts."

"And the others? His friends from the same neighborhood who washed ashore? Did Carlos have a good relationship with them?"

"My son was the one who got them work at Carlos's farm."

Laafrit took down Carlos Gomez's name in his notebook. Now he had an excuse to call his friend in Almería, Luis Fuentes.

The phone rang and Laafrit picked up the receiver. The commissioner asked him to join him in his office immediately.

"Stay calm, uncle. I'll be back in a bit," said Laafrit, casting a look at the old man.

The commissioner accosted Laafrit as soon as his feet hit the office floor.

"Sit down, sit down," he said. "I just had two phone conversations. The first was with Central. They dug up Issa Karami's info. He really does have Spanish citizenship, even though he was born in El Jebha. Before I called you, I talked to my friend, Hajj Mohamed el-Ibrahimi, chief of El Jebha police. He confirmed Issa is well known in town. Issa has agents working for him there and in the regions where marijuana is grown. He said these agents represent Karami in buying crops and turning them into hash while Karami sits pretty in Europe."

"And the second piece of news?" asked Laafrit.

"I got it from the border police. Issa Karami left from the Tangier port last Monday using his Moroccan passport."

"I think we're dealing with an international hash-smuggling syndicate," said Laafrit.

He summed up for the commissioner what he had found out from the victim's father. When he mentioned Carlos Gomez's name, the commissioner cut him off.

"No doubt the victims were just stooges in a huge operation. This Gomez is hiding behind his agriculture business and he's using immigrants for his smuggling operations. I think the scenario's clear now: a boat full of hash took off from our shores with Issa Karami at the helm, while one of Gomez's boats carrying the victims left from the other side. During the handoff in the middle of the Strait, some kind of misunderstanding happened and that's what we're up against now."

"A syndicate with two bosses," said Laafrit. "But we have someone who'll help us get information on the second boss."

"Luis?" asked the commissioner, surprised.

"I'll call him tonight. But there's something else I don't get. When Mohamed Bensallam came back the last time, he didn't stay with his family in Beni Mellal. He spent an entire week in Doukkala and didn't tell anyone why he was going there or what he was doing. I think we've got to check this out."

"I'll ask the Beni Mellal cops to take care of it," said the commissioner.

"Let's wait and see what the rest of the victims' families have to say," said Laafrit after a moment's pause.

"When you've finished with the father," said the commissioner, "send him in to me."

9

LAAFRIT GOT HOME AT EIGHT that night. He was exhausted, and decided he needed to take his mind off the case. He wanted to play the role of the ideal husband since he'd been completely neglecting Naeema these days. So, after dinner, he praised his wife's cooking, cleared the dishes, talked with her about household things, and showed some enthusiasm for repainting the walls. He changed his clothes in the bedroom and played with his daughter until she fell asleep. He then came on to his wife. After they had sex, he took a bath and relaxed in bed under the warm blankets.

Naeema was a few younger than him. They had been students at the university in Rabat. She majored in French literature and he in anthropology. They met by chance at a student protest against the torture of Marxist students. The Moroccan Marxists didn't recognize perestroika or the global fall of Marxism. They were calling for the reform of socialism and an end to imperialism. Naturally, these university protests weren't devoid of a certain amount of romanticism. They were more like parties during which students sang the revolutionary songs of Sheikh Imam, and both men and women would hold hands and sway to the rhythm of oud songs by the activist Said al-Maghribi, who was in exile at the time in France. They'd also read solidarity communiqués and end the parties by repeating the anthem of the Socialist International while holding up pictures of Marx and Lenin.

It was at one of these parties that Khalid Ibrahim, now known as Laafrit, first met Naeema. At that time, he was a senior and she was a freshman. She was dazzled by the atmosphere among the students and delighted by the idea of belonging to something bigger than herself. She was headstrong and excited, repeating slogans from the bottom of her throat and holding hands with her comrades. At the end of the party, she felt a hand still gripping hers. When she tried to let go, Khalid Ibrahim held tight and so she lifted her head toward him. She saw a handsome young man with a Che Guevara beard smiling at her with a revolutionary gentleness.

"This is the first time I've seen you at an activist party," he said to her with delight.

"It's my first year here," she replied, having difficulty extracting her hand from his.

He held her hand tighter.

"It's your first year and you're so enthusiastic!" he said, feigning surprise. "I wonder how you'll be in your senior year . . . probably a leader."

From that day, he insisted on waiting for her in front of the women's dorms, and with an amazing quickness their relationship solidified: they were two comrades brought together to change the world. The conversation among the students was always about politics, class struggle, and the dream of a socialist world free of exploitation. Together, they watched a lot of revolutionary films at the cinema clubs, participated in meetings that lasted until dawn, and played cat and mouse with the police, who broke up their gatherings by force. In all that, they barely left each other's sides, but it wasn't until the end of the year when it was time to say goodbye that they exchanged passionate kisses. Their love was something they assumed without needing to acknowledge it. From the beginning, it was clear Naeema wouldn't have sex with him until their relationship was made official by getting engaged. Despite the liberation of their thinking from a political perspective, the strictures of their conservative traditional upbringing kept them in check.

After Khalid graduated and summer vacation came, they each left Rabat and returned to their homes, Naeema to Tangier and Khalid to Casablanca, though they agreed they'd stay in constant contact.

But this contact didn't last through the summer, let alone until the time came for Naeema to go back for her sophomore year. Khalid Ibrahim disappeared suddenly and news about him broke off. She'd just decided to go to Casablanca to find out about him when that great clash happened between the two student groups, the Marxists and the Islamists, whose movement began to strengthen. These clashes gave the police a pretext to torture all the students, intervening violently. They detained Naeema for an entire week, together with others, at secret police stations. She was subjected to methodical torture to get her to reveal information about her comrades. She was kicked, slapped, pulled by her hair, thrown against the walls, and hung up by her feet for hours. While she was blindfolded, her torturer sexually assaulted her, first by kissing her forcefully, then by squeezing her breasts and grabbing her behind, telling her with disgusting words that she had the choice between his cock in her ass or sitting on a glass bottle. This psychological and physical torture deeply disturbed her. She'd never imagined her political activity was so dangerous or that she'd be punished for it in such a barbaric way.

When they released her, she went straight back to her family. She was in shock but didn't reveal anything of what happened to her. She withdrew into herself and isolated herself in her room, where she preferred to stay in the dark, sitting on the ground and holding her thighs, as if she were afraid. Her father, who was a traditional man (the owner of a clothing store), thought she'd been subjected to an act of black magic and sorcery. As for her mother, she suspected her daughter had been through some sort of emotional shock, in which she might have lost her virginity, and that her lover might have broken up with her.

Her feelings of shock dissipated bit by bit but she never thought about going back to finish her degree and she refused all her suitors. She spent all her time on the couch, watching TV series or reading women's magazines. She took no interest in her appearance and put on the hijab, though she had no deep religious convictions. She never thought she'd see Khalid Ibrahim again. She stopped thinking about him completely and didn't even recognize him when she found him standing at her door one day.

Over a number of conversations, he told her what had happened. His father had died and his family didn't have any way to get by unless he provided for them. He felt he had to get a job as fast as possible, so he took the police academy test and became an inspector. He took the job even though he was overqualified. He said he was ashamed of himself at the beginning and that he felt he'd betrayed his principles, which held the police as nothing more than torturers and guardians for the privileges of the rich. He buried his head in his hands and confessed he'd been ashamed to look for her out of fear she'd think he'd committed a crime against their beliefs, especially when some of his friends found out she'd been arrested and subjected to barbaric torture. He then praised the reforms that'd happened in the political system and convinced her that the years of lead—the decades of human rights abuses in Morocco—had ended and that his acceptance into the police academy, despite his past political activities, proved the country had entered a new phase, cutting a path toward democracy and human rights. He tried to convince her the police stations were cleansed of torture and that even though he was in the police, he was still an activist at heart and was bent on applying the law. He said he refused all bribes and took no part in the pilfering that went on. And, at that moment, he asked her to marry him, declaring his love for her and saying that the only reason he'd asked to work in Tangier was so he could be close to her.

For Laafrit, Naeema was a gift from heaven. She embodied the captivating Andalusian beauty that distinguishes the women of the north. But after marrying her, he began to feel that she was too sensitive. She'd start crying at the drop of a hat. At times, he'd get annoyed that she couldn't let go of that terrible week she'd spent at the police station, and whenever they had a fight she'd see a kind of mockery of fate in her marriage to a cop. Their relationship got so tense that they split up after a year of marriage, but their families intervened to reconcile them. Naeema felt she wouldn't be happy even if she married someone else and that her experience of arrest, torture, abuse, and humiliation was a deep wound that'd never heal. No one understood this, of course, and everyone thought all her problems would be solved if she only got pregnant. Fate smiled on her, and indeed everything changed once she had Reem.

For his part, Laafrit was focused on his profession more than his personal life. Because he was working so hard and showed an unexpected aptitude for his job, he got promoted to detective in record time. But this was at the expense of his family life, since he was spending all his time at work and would usually come home drunk. Naeema started worrying he wasn't satisfied with just drinking and that maybe he was cheating on her. Nonetheless, she tried as hard as possible to rid herself of her anxiety and to make their daughter the center of her life.

Later that night, Laafrit went into the living room and sat down in his lounge chair. He sat there in the dark and didn't feel like turning on the TV. He was enjoying the peace and quiet, but his cop nature forced him to start putting together what the shooting victim's father had said earlier that day.

Laafrit thought the most intriguing aspect of the story was that Mohamed Bensallam came to Beni Mellal four times in the span of only a year. Laafrit then wondered about Bensallam's marriage and how he'd managed to buy a house. Where'd Bensallam gotten the money for all that if it wasn't from smuggling hash?

Laafrit tried to go over the case from the beginning: four bodies washed up in three days, the last one shot four times. The bullets indicated the kind of gun used to kill Bensallam, which happened to be the same kind found in Issa Karami's apartment in Martil. As for Karami, he had a Spanish passport and belonged to the "new generation" of hash dealers.

Investigations showed all the victims were living on the other side, in Spain, and were all doing farm work in Almería for a man named Carlos Gomez. Bensallam was the only one who'd gotten papers. The others were illegals. The last time Bensallam came back to Morocco, he spent a week in the Doukkala region without telling anyone why he went there.

Laafrit licked his lips, craving a lozenge, but in an attempt to keep it from becoming a habit, he'd promised himself not to have them at home.

Up till now, Laafrit thought everything was proceeding clearly and that the key to the investigation had to center on a meeting between the victims and Issa Karami. In the long run, he told himself, it's a case about hash. His best guess was that the four victims had set out on a boat from the Spanish side while another boat set out from Moroccan shores carrying hash. This meant the coast guard either turned a blind eye or simply hadn't noticed anything.

But why had Karami shot only Bensallam? Why had he put his jacket back on him after killing him, especially when he was simply going to toss him into the sea? Was it to divert attention? And why'd Karami left the gun at his house without the least precaution? Did the choice of the four victims, all from the same neighborhood in Beni Mellal, have any significance?

The coroner's report established that the victims hadn't eaten the same last meal. Bensallam's was varied and gourmet while the others' was miserable and cheap. So where'd the meeting taken place? Before the attempted deal? Was Carlos Gomez a big-time smuggler hiding behind his agriculture business? Were the victims only stooges in an international syndicate, just like the commissioner said?

These questions swirled in Laafrit's head before he called his friend Luis Fuentes, the Spanish detective in Almería. It had been a long time since they talked. Laafrit remembered all the good times they'd had together in Tangier when Luis was working for the Spanish DEA. He came to Morocco as part of bilateral cooperation to fight this plague and as evidence the Spanish were standing in solidarity with all the efforts that Morocco was exerting. His team was concentrating on some Spanish truck drivers who were complaining they were victims after getting caught transporting drugs. The plan was not to arrest them until after they penetrated the network. Laafrit was chosen for this job on the Moroccan side since he spoke fluent Spanish, and Luis got the job for the same reason: he spoke fluent Arabic.

Luis was Moroccan by birth. He was born in El Hoceima and left for Spain when he was seven. As he told Laafrit, his father loved to hunt. He used to dedicate all his time to it, going out with friends from the Rif Mountains. For this reason alone, Luis's father insisted on staying in Morocco but Luz, Luis's mother, felt that if they stayed, she'd never regain her husband's attention. She'd simply become one of "the Moroccan women" whose job it was to cook, clean, and raise the kids. So in order to get her husband away from his second wife, hunting, Luz asked him to go back to Spain. But he stubbornly refused. Her only choice was to take the kids and go back to Almería, her native city. Luis's father was determined to resist his wife, so he stayed on in El Hoceima for three years, alone on his farm, until loneliness got the better of him and he went back to his family. Even now, Luis told Laafrit, the man continued to live on the memories of those bygone days in Morocco.

Laafrit smiled to himself as he remembered Luis's infatuation with Fifi. When Luis went to see her show, he'd turn into a different person. He'd jump onto the dance floor and shake his hips as he danced in front of her, making people laugh. Luis wasn't drunk. He was just giving his emotions free rein and letting loose. If Laafrit hadn't warned Fifi about Luis the first time and told her not to get too involved with him, Luis definitely would've gotten carried away coming and going between Almería and Tangier just to see her.

Laafrit looked at his watch. It was 10:15, which meant it was now 11:15 in Spain. Was it too late to call? It didn't matter. How many times had Luis called him after midnight Moroccan time? He took five minutes to collect his thoughts and then dialed the number. After the third ring, Luis picked up.

"Sí," Laafrit heard him say in a soft voice.

"Sorry if I disturbed you," said Laafrit in perfect Spanish.

"Who's this . . . ?" asked Luis, surprised. "Laafrit?"

"Sorry," said Laafrit. "I forgot the time difference."

"We might as well be on your time here," he said in Arabic, letting out a laugh. "How are you?"

"Good," responded Laafrit in Spanish. "And you? How are things over there?"

"Great," said Luis in Arabic.

"So," said Laafrit, "I won't keep you long. I'm busy these days with a tough case. Half of it's here and the other half's over there in Almería. Maybe I can tell you the details quickly."

Laafrit summarized the case in a few sentences. Luis interrupted him when he mentioned Carlos Gomez.

"Carlos Gomez," said Luis in Arabic, "is a friend of my father. He's crazy about hunting too. He's probably the biggest farmer in Andalusia. He alone exports enough tomatoes for all the European markets—more than your entire country does. It's impossible he has the slightest connection to hash or the smuggler you mentioned."

"And the others?" asked Laafrit.

"Give me their names."

Laafrit told Luis about all the victims, concentrating on the name of Mohamed Bensallam, the one who was shot dead and had legal papers. Luis wrote the names down quickly.

"Got it. I'll call you back as soon as I have something. Tell me," Luis said, letting out a slight laugh, "have you seen Fifi recently?"

"I saw her this week," said Laafrit. "She asked about you and told me to say hello."

"I won't ever forget those nights . . . oh!" said Luis, sighing audibly.

"We'll talk more about Fifi when it's on your dime," said Laafrit, cutting him off.

"If I were in Tangier," said Luis joking, "I'd get dressed right now and head over to the Macarena! How can you sleep when Fifi's so close? What's wrong with you?"

Luis chuckled and then hung up.

Laafrit spent all day Sunday with his family, something he hadn't done in a long time. He suggested to Naeema that they have lunch at a pizza restaurant owned by one of his friends. Outside, he took her by the arm and clung to her. She hid what she could of her face so he couldn't see her annoyance. She knew he felt burdened and that he was holding on to her only out of a heavy sense of guilt for being gone so much these days.

At ten o'clock Sunday night, the phone rang. Laafrit picked up after the first ring.

"Good evening," said Luis in Arabic. "Seems you were waiting by the phone for my call."

"Didn't we agree on this time?" Laafrit asked, in Arabic as well, playing along with Luis's desire to speak the language.

"You robbed me of my weekend, my friend," said Luis.

"What'd you find out?" Laafrit asked as his heart began to pound.

"Mohamed Bensallam—I've confirmed his identity. He really did have residence papers and Carlos was the one who got them for him. Like I told you before, my father hunts with Carlos so he got to know Bensallam. Whenever my father met him, they chatted in Arabic."

"How does Carlos explain Bensallam's disappearance?"

"I put my father on it but Carlos didn't tell him anything more than that he fired Bensallam. He refused to say why."

"Did your father tell him we discovered Bensallam's body here in Tangier?"

"No, I told him to keep it secret. My father thought it was strange Carlos fired Bensallam so suddenly. Only a few days before, he saw the two of them eating dinner together at a restaurant and laughing like old friends. My father was surprised to see them all buddy-buddy, since he knew Carlos is such a racist. Carlos hates immigrants and exploits them shamefully on his farm."

Laafrit remembered what they found in Bensallam's stomach after the autopsy.

"If they were eating salad, paella, and chocolate flan with lots of red wine, then that was Mohamed Bensallam's last supper," said Laafrit.

Luis laughed but he stopped suddenly.

"Did you analyze his stomach contents?" he asked.

"Yeah, but the others only had mixed vegetables and bread."

Luis was silent for a moment. Laafrit took the opportunity to ask him about something else.

"Does Carlos own some kind of boat?"

"Carlos has a bunch of fishing boats," responded Luis. "But they're all dry docked now because your country hasn't renewed its fishing agreement with ours. Carlos is a big investor in both land and sea," he said in jest.

"About how old is he?"

"So I've become your top informant?" asked Luis, laughing. "Carlos is the same age as my father, about sixty-five. He has three sons and two daughters. One of his daughters is married to the most famous lawyer in Madrid and the other lives in Israel. As for his sons, they live in Almería and they all work for him. The youngest is twenty and the oldest is my age."

"I know it's on your dime," said Laafrit, "so I'm sorry to keep you on the phone. Did you find anything out about the other three?"

"The others," said Luis in a taut voice, "they're the ones who took up my whole weekend. I don't know why your young people keep risking their lives to come here to live in a trash dump. A few kilometers from Almería, near the fields, there are hundreds of Moroccans who made it to paradise and now live in squats and cardboard boxes without water, electricity, or plumbing. They drink river water, burn candles for light, and crap outside. They spend their days working in the fields and come back at night to their shit holes. I spent all day Sunday there wandering around, asking about those four who disappeared. I kept getting the same response: that they left for Madrid."

"Did you tell them you're a cop?"

"No. You know I'm doing this outside my jurisdiction. I wanted to keep it secret. Besides, if anyone knew I was sticking my nose in illegal immigration, I'd get some unwanted attention from the farm owners. Even some friends in the force would start getting curious."

"The situation's that serious?" asked Laafrit, astonished.

"That's another story," said Luis. "In short, the big farm owners here buy the silence of the cops so they'll turn a blind eye on illegal immigrants. That's why it's easy for these farm owners to hire illegals at the lowest possible rate and make them work long hours in medieval conditions."

"By the way," said Laafrit, "I forgot to tell you about a guy who was friends with them and from the same city. I got his name when I questioned the victims' families. Jaouad Benmousa. Maybe he's still there in that camp."

Luis wrote the name down.

"Tell me, what kind of gun was used to kill Bensallam?"

"A Beretta nine-millimeter."

"What're you doing to catch Issa Karami?"

"Central's dealing with that now. They're coordinating with Interpol."

"And what about the shooting victim?"

"Mohamed Bensallam," said Laafrit. "There's still something I don't get about him. When he came back to Morocco the last time, he stayed in Beni Mellal for only one day and then went to the Doukkala region. He didn't tell anyone where he was going or why."

"I read an article in *El País* about a disease that struck your tomato crops in that area," said Luis.

"Our papers have been talking about it every day."

"Don't forget this is on my tab," said Luis.

"Sorry," said Laafrit. "Look for Jaouad Benmousa. Maybe he can help us with this. Next time, I'll be the one who calls you. Thanks again."

"If I get anything new," said Luis before hanging up, "it'll be me calling."

10

It took a lot to convince the commissioner it was necessary for Laafrit to travel all the way to Beni Mellal. As far as the commissioner was concerned, it was enough to have a detective there finish up the investigation, since most of the elements of the case had been cracked. The commissioner thought all the important details would be revealed once they arrested the killer.

Nonetheless, Laafrit insisted, so he left Tangier at eight o'clock Tuesday morning, driving south on the main highway. He got to Casablanca at eleven and after a half-hour break, he set out toward Beni Mellal. At exactly two in the afternoon, he was in the middle of the city.

Laafrit had never been to Beni Mellal before. All he knew about it was that the city was famous for the Ouzoud waterfalls. He had lunch in a cheap restaurant and then took a drive around the city. Compared to Tangier, this place seemed like a different world, with donkey carts sharing the road with cars. But as soon as Laafrit got out toward the outskirts of the city, he couldn't resist stopping and wandering around. It overlooked incredibly beautiful scenery, with green fields extending like an ocean as far as the eye could see.

At three in the afternoon, Laafrit headed to the police station, where he met Commissioner Bouchta. From his accent, Laafrit knew the man was from the north, despite all the sounds and words he'd picked up from working in the interior. Instead of "fum," the word for "mouth," he said "dqum" as he told Laafrit how the face of one of the victims' mothers became partially paralyzed from grief. The commissioner also told Laafrit about the solemn funeral for the four young men that almost turned into a big protest. He hinted in a roundabout way it hadn't been necessary for Laafrit to come—conducting a routine investigation didn't warrant a six-hundred-kilometer trip. A detective from Beni Mellal could have handled it.

When the commissioner finally set Laafrit free, he was surprised to find Detective Said Lamoursi, an old colleague from Tangier. The two men embraced warmly.

"What're you doing here in Beni Mellal? Why didn't you tell me you were coming?" asked Said.

"Maybe you just ignored the email I sent so you wouldn't have to host me," Laafrit joked.

"Shame on you, my friend," said Said disapprovingly.

"I'm here because of the dead harraga," said Laafrit. "Can you show me where Mohamed Bensallam's family lives?"

"Mohamed Bensallam. If I remember correctly, he's the one who was shot dead?"

"Yeah. I want to talk with his wife."

"Is that all you want with her?" asked Said with a wink.

"I've already talked with his father in Tangier," said Laafrit, ignoring Said's comment.

Once outside, Laafrit insisted they take his car. Laafrit drove as Said gave him directions.

"How long ago did you start working here?" asked Laafrit.

"This has been my city since the day I left Tangier."

"I didn't know you were a Mellali," said Laafrit.

The car came to a complete stop in a street jam-packed with pedestrians. A groom's huge marriage offering was on its way to his bride. An ox pulled a cart carrying clothes, sugar cakes, a bag of wheat, and boxes of olives, dates, sweets, and henna. Behind the cart was a group of musicians taking up the entire road, with women dancing and trilling. Laafrit laughed as he looked at the women dancing in the middle of the street.

"Is this all that happens in Beni Mellal?" asked Laafrit in jest.

"What do you think?" asked Said, smiling. "You're not in Tangier any more, my friend."

"Only in Beni Mellal," said Laafrit. "Say, since you're from here, do you know anything about Bensallam?"

"He doesn't have a criminal record."

"That I know," said Laafrit. "What are people saying?"

Said didn't answer. The road finally emptied out and the Fiat moved slowly as Laafrit tried to avoid the potholes. Said told Laafrit to turn onto a road, and they drove up to a two-story house.

They got out of the car and walked up to the front door. After Said rang the bell, a woman dressed in white came to greet them. She had the face of a teenager and couldn't have been more than twenty. Said smiled at her as if they already knew each other.

"This is Amina, the wife of the deceased," said Said. "And this is a detective from Tangier. He's here to ask you some questions."

"May God bestow patience on you," said Laafrit, feigning as much grief as he could.

He noticed through the open door the house was full of people and he could hear weeping. The family must still be holding vigil and receiving guests.

"Come in," said Amina. "I'll take you to the room where the men are sitting."

"Please," said Laafrit, "I came all the way from Tangier just to ask you some questions. If there isn't a suitable place here for us to talk, you could come with us to the station. I won't take up much of your time."

Hesitation appeared on Amina's face. She turned into the house.

"Isn't there an empty room where we could talk?" asked Laafrit. "We'd like to spare you the trouble of coming with us downtown."

"We could go upstairs," she said nervously.

She went inside and opened a door on the right.

"Please," she said, clearly uncomfortable. "I'll tell the others and then join you."

Laafrit glanced around the house. It looked like a little tomb. The ceiling was decorated with plaster engravings and the walls had ornate tiles surrounded by marble borders. The bare floor was inlaid with mosaics. The doors were made of beautiful hand-carved wood. Laafrit guessed the house had four bedrooms in addition to the big living room.

"How much is a house like this here in Beni Mellal?" he asked, turning to Said.

"A lot . . . maybe sixty, seventy thousand for the whole thing," he said, looking around.

Laafrit heard a bunch of people walk upstairs. He turned around and saw Amina with a group of people behind her.

"I don't want any gossip," he whispered to Said. "Keep the others downstairs. Do your best to console them."

Laafrit followed Amina into the room, looking at her closely. He sat down opposite her.

"As you know, I'm the detective charged with investigating your husband's murder. At the moment, we have a suspect whose name is Issa Karami. Have you heard that name before?"

Amina looked confused and put a pillow on her knees. She gripped it and shook her head.

"When did you meet your husband?"

She blushed.

"We were neighbors in the area around the mosque. After he went to Spain, his mother would visit us a lot and she'd tell me: 'Grow up quickly so you can be my son's wife.' When he got his Spanish papers, he proposed and last summer we got married."

"During the past year," said Laafrit, "he came back to Morocco four times, right?"

"Yes, four times."

"Did he stay with you here in Beni Mellal or go somewhere else?"

"He stayed with his family. We were still engaged."

"Do you know any close friends of his?"

She appeared to pause to think, but didn't respond.

"Did he have a lot of friends?"

"I don't know. Once we got engaged, we'd spend the whole day together. At night, we'd each sleep at home with our families."

"And after your marriage?"

"After we got married, we lived together for only . . . only a month. After that, he went back to work."

"Where did you spend that month together?"

"In El Jadida. We rented a beach house there."

"Just the two of you?"

"My husband's family and my younger sister came with us."

"Did your husband spend the entire month there with you?"

Amina seemed confused. Laafrit noticed she kept twisting her wedding ring around her finger.

"He was gone for two or three days and then came back."

"Where did he go?"

"He didn't tell me."

"Did you press him?"

Amina let out a deep sigh.

"Yes, I did, because we got into fights about these trips."

"Did you have any doubts about him?"

Amina looked away from Laafrit and lowered her head.

"He swore he was faithful, but on his last trip here he told me he hadn't come from Spain to see me. He came back for something else."

"What was it?" asked Laafrit, his eyes widening.

"He's dead now," said Amina, on the verge of tears. "We shouldn't speak ill of the dead."

"We ask for compassion and forgiveness for him," said Laafrit. "But we have to know the truth. You said he came home for some other reason. What was it?"

"The last time he was here," Amina said, as tears ran from her eyes, "he didn't stay with me for a single night. He didn't touch me. He arrived in the morning and left after lunch. He disappeared for a week and when he came back, he stayed with me for less than an hour and then left again for Spain."

"Where did he go for that week?"

"I . . . I suspect he had a relationship with another woman."

"Do you know who this woman is?"

"When we were in El Jadida, I caught him more than once with a woman named Hanan. He told me she was a friend from college but I suspect he had an affair with her."

"Does this Hanan live in El Jadida?"

"Yes."

"Do you know her address?"

"No."

Laafrit felt he'd plunged her deeper than he should have into an old sea of turbulent emotions.

"Okay," he said. "Did you ever ask your husband where he got the money to buy this house?"

"Why would I ask him something like that?" she asked, confused. "Everyone who works abroad buys a house."

Laafrit smiled and felt an urge for a lozenge.

"Did he come back the last time by car?"

"A Mercedes 190."

"Didn't you press him to know where he went?"

"He said he had some work and wouldn't say a word more. He was evading talking about it."

"When he came back, didn't you ask him again?"

"He only stayed with me for an hour. He was in a rush and he said he had to get back to Almería that day."

"Was he afraid of something?"

"He was in a rush. His mind was elsewhere."

"Would he call you from Almería?"

"About once a month."

"And when he was here in Morocco that week, did he call you?"

"He called a few hours before he got here."

"Didn't you ask him where he was calling from?"

"Yes. He said he was in Oualidia but I knew he was lying. He was probably with that woman in El Jadida."

All of a sudden, Laafrit stopped talking. He tried to come up with more questions for the woman but nothing worthwhile came to mind. He then thought the intimacy of the bedroom usually leads men to reveal some secrets, or at least to allude to them. But the situation was different in this case. The reason might be that Bensallem hadn't lived with his wife for that long.

"Fine," he said with a kind of resignation. "Did your husband leave any personal things here? Papers, clothes, anything else?"

Amina didn't seem to understand at first.

"He left some clothes he didn't use any more," she said after a pause. "He has his own drawer in our wardrobe where he put old photos from when he was in college and some letters."

Laafrit gave her a smile.

"Would you mind if I had a look at them?"

Without responding, she put the pillow aside and got up. Laafrit followed her into the bedroom. Amina pulled the wardrobe doors open. Most of the clothes were Amina's except for a shelf with men's shirts, socks, and underwear. Laafrit felt silly standing there next to Amina in front of her open wardrobe.

She looked down at a single locked drawer.

"The key was always with him," she said. "Sorry."

Laafrit looked at the lock. It would be easy to break.

"Do you mind?" he asked, gripping the drawer.

She shook her head, and Laafrit yanked the drawer open. Just as Amina had said, Laafrit found a photo album inside. He flipped through it quickly. He also found an expensive wristwatch, a few old letters, Bensallam's old college ID, and some other knickknacks.

What caught Laafrit's attention was a plastic box. When he opened it, he found a number of small vials like those sold in pharmacies, especially for injections. The vials were sealed shut and contained a dark liquid. There were no names or labels on them. Laafrit held one up to Amina.

"What's this?" he asked.

"I don't know," she said, pursing her lips.

"Ever seen these before?"

She shook her head.

"No idea what's inside them?"

"No."

"Did your husband have some kind of illness?"

She shook her head again.

Laafrit took all the vials out. At the bottom of the box he found a folded sheet of paper that had been crumpled and then smoothed out again. An illegible word was written on the paper. There were some rough marks next to some words scrawled in French. Next to one of the marks, Laafrit read "Oualidia."

"When your husband called you last, he said he was calling from Oualidia?"

"Yes, but I thought he was really calling from El Jadida," she said.

Laafrit put the vials back in the box and stuck the paper in his pocket.

"I'm taking these with me," he said.

Amina didn't seem to care. She shrugged as if the whole thing didn't have anything to do with her.

"Do you have a recent picture of your husband?"

She took the photo album out of the wardrobe and flipped through it.

"These are all pictures from our wedding," she said in frustration. She was looking for a picture of her husband alone.

"Can I have one of the wedding pictures?" asked Laafrit, stopping her.

"I'll keep it as a souvenir," he added, trying to make light of the situation, although they both knew why he needed the picture.

He looked at the photo and was struck by Amina's beauty. She was standing next to Bensallam in his tux, wearing a white wedding dress and smiling happily at the photographer.

Back at the Beni Mellal police station, Laafrit put the plastic box on the desk and took out a vial. He opened it up, sniffed it,, and then gave it to Detective Said, who was sitting in front of him.

"I found these vials in Bensallam's locked drawer in his bedroom. There's no label and his wife doesn't know anything about them."

Said looked closely at the vial, opened it, and put a drop on his finger.

"Don't taste it," said Laafrit, grinning. "Might be poison."

"Looks to me like the stuff herb doctors sell to boost sex drive."

Laafrit laughed. He spread out the sheet he found with the vials and began to sound out the roughly scrawled place names: Oualidia, Chtouka, Bir Jdid, Haouzia.

He pushed the sheet toward Said.

"This was with the vials in the box."

Said looked at it.

"It's a map of the Doukkala region," he said immediately.

Laafrit realized he heard that name a lot these days.

"I found it under the vials in the box. Amina remembered Bensallem called her from Oualidia last time he came back to Morocco."

"It's just a local aphrodisiac," said Said in jest. "Sold only in the rural markets. Maybe Bensallam went from village to village looking for it."

"If that's right," said Laafrit, faking a laugh, "we're going to have to redo the autopsy to confirm he was impotent."

"Why bother looking at the corpse? Just go ask his wife!" said Said.

With all his guesses and jokes, Laafrit felt Said's involvement was pointless. He put the vials back in the box and stuck the sheet in his pocket. He looked at his watch, pretending to be in a rush.

"I've got a long trip ahead of me," said Laafrit.

Said got up gently, as if he was afraid Laafrit was trying to get away.

"I swear to God," said Said, "I told my family you're going to be our guest tonight. You can't just leave like that."

"You're right," said Laafrit without putting up resistance, realizing Said was going to insist no matter what. "Why rush? I still have plenty of time to make it back to Tangier."

And with that he sat back down again.

"So, is this town famous for any good food?" he asked playfully.

"Our city is famous for the proverb that goes 'the guest doesn't ask for anything but the owner of the house takes good care of him.' But I like you, so I'll top the proverb and do whatever you ask," said Said.

Laafrit smiled and took out a fresh box of lozenges. He gave a lozenge to Said and then put one in his mouth.

11

LAAFRIT COULDN'T RESIST THE URGE to go check things out in Oualidia, despite how many times he told himself it'd be a complete waste of time. So, at seven the next morning, he said good-bye to Said and told him he was heading back to Tangier. But now here he was, more than a hundred kilometers farther south, even though he was still thinking about changing direction and heading north.

His consolation was that he was soothing his policeman's curiosity, something that was hard for him to control. Wherever he looked from the car window, he saw lush green becoming gradually paler as if it were dissipating. Then it became dense again with the beginning of new fields. Laafrit loved the rose, white, scarlet, and yellow sparkling like lilies in the midst of the green. From time to time he looked up from the wheel at the summer sky, which was clear blue in every direction.

He had a quick lunch in El Jadida. After another half hour on the road, he arrived at Oualidia. He remembered camping on the beach there with some friends twenty years ago. What remained in his mind about this area was that it had a great campsite and thick woods overlooking the sea from rocky hills. At this time of year, he was sure Oualidia would be empty except for locals. Laafrit thought this would really help his chances to find someone who'd met Bensallem, especially since Bensallam, according to his wife, visited Oualidia at a time when there weren't any summer tourists around.

The Fiat stopped in front of a café with a wide terrace crowded with people. Laafrit squeezed the car between two four-by-fours. As he got out he noticed a cop car, as well as a car with the logo of the Moroccan TV station 2M. Sitting at a table on the patio, he ordered a coffee and checked out the people around him. He recognized some of the station's journalists. He also saw a TV camera and some other gear sitting on top of the tables. He gathered from what he heard that the TV people were there because of the epidemic that had struck the region's tomato harvest.

The waiter brought Laafrit's coffee and looked at him suspiciously, as you would a stranger in a small town. Laafrit gave him a wide smile and took out the photo Amina had given him. He bent it in half so the bride was at the back and the groom, dressed in his neat tux, was in front.

"Excuse me," Laafrit said, presenting the photo to the waiter. "This man was here a few weeks ago. Did you see him?"

The waiter looked at Laafrit skeptically before checking out the photo. The detective watched the waiter's reaction carefully and thought from his suspicious looks the waiter would be lying if he denied it. All of a sudden, the waiter turned the photo over and let out a laugh when he saw the bride.

"Did the guy run off on his wedding night?" he asked.

Laafrit gave him a smile.

"Yeah, he was at the café," added the waiter. "He drove a Mercedes 190 with Spanish plates."

Laafrit's heart was pounding, and he tried not to come across like a cop.

"Fantastic," he said, emboldened. "Yeah, he's the one with the Mercedes with Spanish plates. You guys eat a lot of fish here, so your memory's really good. Tell me, did you notice the woman with him?"

The waiter looked to the right and left as if he were looking for someone.

"He didn't have a woman with him. He was sitting with Si Lahsan."

"Oh, Si Lahsan," said Laafrit, laughing loudly. "Where's he?"

"Over there," said the waiter. "With the TV people."

"Remind me," said Laafrit, putting his hand on his temple. "Si Lahsan is . . ."

"The agricultural engineer," said the waiter, not picking up on Laafrit's charade. "That's him in the black leather jacket."

"Oh yeah," said Laafrit, taking back the photo.

The waiter heard someone calling him so he went back into the café without paying attention to Laafrit, who was thanking him.

Meanwhile, the TV director was giving instructions to the cameraman while the journalist, who was standing next to one of the farmers, adjusted his necktie and tested the microphone. Like the other people there, Laafrit got up and stood behind the guy carrying the TV camera. His eyes were on Si Lahsan, who was getting ready to give an interview. The director gave the signal to begin, but before the journalist even finished his question the farmer burst out yelling.

"Everything's lost! Not a single good tomato is left. Last year we suffered from the whitefly, and this year we've got an epidemic and we don't know how it infected us, despite all our precautions. More than twenty thousand wasted! I've got debts and the banks have no mercy. We're asking the state for help. We're demanding that the government step in!"

The man was yelling as if he were leading a protest. Other farmers spoke in front of the camera with the same pain and distress. Then came Si Lahsan's turn. He spoke in such a low voice that Laafrit could only make out a few words from where he was standing.

The farmers soon got into a loud argument. Laafrit was waiting for a chance to get the engineer alone. As soon as the journalist moved away from the group, Laafrit walked up to Si Lahsan and greeted him as if they knew each other.

"Hey, Si Lahsan, how's it going?"

"Good," replied the engineer, looking at Laafrit suspiciously.

Si Lahsan was about forty. He hadn't shaved in a week. His hair was long and curly and his eyes looked worn out. Laafrit gently pulled him by the arm away from the others.

"If you don't mind," said Laafrit, "I'd like to talk a little about Mohamed Bensallam."

The engineer suddenly lost his gentle appearance. He clearly wasn't thrilled with Laafrit.

"Who are you?" asked Si Lahsan tensely.

Laafrit knew the act he'd used with the waiter wouldn't work with the engineer. He decided to be up front from the start.

"I'm a detective from Tangier."

"Nice to meet you," said Si Lahsan suspiciously. "Can I see your ID?"

"You're right to ask," said the detective.

Laafrit showed his ID to the engineer, who wasn't satisfied with just glancing at it. Si Lahsan took the ID, read everything on it, and then gave it back to Laafrit with a cautious smile on his face.

He took the photo out of his pocket and instead of handing it to the engineer with the groom facing upward, Laafrit accidentally showed him the bride.

"Have you met the person in the photograph before?" he asked, starting his questioning in an official tone.

The engineer laughed out loud. Laafrit looked at the photo and quickly turned it over.

"Sorry, sorry," he said.

"Strange," said the engineer, looking quickly at the photo. "He didn't tell me he was married."

"Can you please tell me the name of the person in the photo?" asked Laafrit.

"Mohamed Bensallam," said the engineer. "Did something happen to him?"

"When did you meet him?"

"In November, but why all the questions? I want to know why you're interrogating me."

"I'll explain everything," said Laafrit gently. "But please, answer my questions first. When did you meet Bensallam for the first time?"

"Like I said, in November. I found him wandering around in the tomato fields and when he found out I was an agricultural engineer, he told me he was a student at the agriculture school in Madrid. He said he was preparing a thesis on irrigation. On the economics of the irrigation water used in vegetable farming in general and in tomato farming in particular."

The engineer noticed the look of surprise on Laafrit's face.

"Please go on," said the detective.

"I gave him some help. I took him to the irrigation canals and showed him the pumps controlling them."

"How long was he here in Oualidia?"

"Two days, I think."

"Was he alone?"

"Yeah. He spent the day here but the night in El Jadida."

"Had you ever see him before November?"

"No, I don't think so."

"I asked the waiter and he told me he saw you two together at the café."

"That's right, we were there a few times."

"Did he tell you about his personal life?"

"We talked about ordinary things," replied the engineer after hesitating for a moment. "About his studies in Spain and his life in Madrid. I don't remember him telling me anything exciting or memorable."

The TV cars were getting ready to leave.

"Si Lahsan!" yelled one of the journalists, sounding the horn.

"If you don't mind, I've got to go with the TV crew to the tomato fields," said the engineer apologetically.

"Mind if I go with you?" asked Laafrit.

"Sure. I'd like to know what's behind all these questions."

Laafrit got into the engineer's old Renault 4. The line of cars set out quickly on a dirt road to make the forty-kilometer trip. As they drove, Laafrit told the engineer all about the case, from the day the bodies washed ashore to when they found the gun at the suspect's apartment, and then his conversation with the Spanish detective. When Laafrit mentioned the name Carlos Gomez, the engineer cut him off.

"Carlos Gomez's company in Almería," he said in surprise, "is the one that supplied the Daniella tomato seedlings from Israel to one of the Moroccan importers in the El Oulja region."

"Are those the seedlings that caused all the problems?" asked Laafrit.

"Last year, yes. The Daniella seedlings carried TYLCV, the tomato yellow leaf curl virus, which is spread by very small insects that look like flies. They're called *Bemisia tabaci*. Thank God, we did everything we could to get rid of it but this year's disaster has destroyed so many crops you can't even imagine. It destroyed thousands of hectares and, despite all our analyses, we still don't know the slightest thing about it."

"Couldn't it be the seedlings?"

"No way. We banned the importation of the Daniella seedlings, conducted the necessary tests, and even made use of foreign labs. It's been confirmed that all the seedlings we used this year were virus free, but this current wave of the disease has spread like the plague."

They had slowed down so much the other cars disappeared from sight. Laafrit and the engineer exchanged glances. It seemed as if they wanted to say the same thing.

"What do you think was Bensallam's motive for posing as an agriculture student and coming here?" asked Laafrit.

"That's what I was wondering. It seems strange Bensallam was working for the owner of the biggest tomato-exporting company in Spain. Carlos Gomez's company was the intermediary for Moroccan farmers who imported the seedlings carrying TYLCV last year."

"Don't you think Bensallam was sent here by Gomez?"

"Maybe. Gomez might've sent him to spy."

Laafrit took out the sheet of paper he had found in Bensallam's house in the box of vials. He asked the engineer to pull over for a second. The engineer stopped in the middle of the road, took the sheet from the detective, and began looking at it closely.

"Oualidia, El Oulja, Azemmour, Chtouka, Bir Jdid, Haouzia," he read aloud.

The engineer moved the sheet away and looked at it with growing surprise.

"It's a map of Doukkala," said Laafrit.

"No," said the engineer. "It's a map of tomato farming in Doukkala. This guy must have been a spy for Gomez," he said, turning to Laafrit.

"Couldn't Bensallam have some connection with what's happening here?" asked Laafrit after a moment.

"What do you mean? The epidemic? I don't think so. Anything that could've infected the tomatoes would've come from seedlings, and seedlings imported in huge quantities. This operation's now under heavy supervision. Big companies control it. Bensallam was probably just sent to spy."

"Possibly," said Laafrit. "But maybe he told you he was researching the economics of water irrigation to distract you from his real interest in the tomatoes."

"Maybe," said the engineer.

Si Lahsan gave the sheet of paper back to the detective and started the car. The old Renault took off, leaving a cloud dust behind it.

When they reached the tomato fields, Laafrit was stunned by the sheer size of the cultivated area.

"I thought all the tomatoes for export were grown in hothouses," said Laafrit.

"We have five hundred hectares of hothouses spread out over a number of areas, and another thousand hectares of open tomato fields between Oualidia, Chtouka, Bir Jdid, and Haouzia. Those are the areas Bensallam drew on his map, the same ones completely destroyed by the epidemic."

The engineer pulled up next to the other cars. The TV crew was getting ready to shoot the fields. The director approached Si Lahsan and spoke to him as if Laafrit wasn't there.

"If you don't mind, after we take some panoramic shots of the fields, we'll ask you to give a scientific commentary for viewers."

The engineer nodded in agreement. Laafrit walked into the tomato fields, which were devastated as far as the eye could see. The leaves had wilted and turned a pale yellow. Only at this point did Laafrit understand the true scope of the catastrophe.

"As you can see," said the engineer, pointing across the fields, "all plant medicines and insecticides are useless against this new epidemic."

The director came back with his crew and asked Si Lahsan to walk deep into the fields. As the soundman put the small microphone on the engineer's jacket collar, Laafrit moved away and stood behind the camera, next to the others. The director gave the signal to begin and the engineer picked up a tomato plant and began his commentary.

"The virus that struck the region last year curled and yellowed the tomato leaves. It was spread by an insect called the whitefly. It's very small—between 1.6 and 2.67 millimeters—and feasts on the sap of tomato plants. It breeds and lays nearly three hundred eggs at a time. The fly's gestation from egg to full-grown insect takes about four weeks. With the help of winds, it crosses long distances. It's possible for the mature insect to infect plants with the virus for a period of up to ten days. Last year we managed to quarantine the fly, and this year we took precautionary measures and used every available means, from insecticide to nets and flytraps. We destroyed the damaged plants, uprooted infected shrubs, and burned the rest of the tomatoes and plants. We also completely banned the importation of Daniella seedlings, which were supplied by the Banfort Company. Unfortunately, we still don't understand this new disease, which couldn't possibly have come from the seedlings. There's a committee at the ministerial level following the situation's developments, working with producers, and watching over the lab analyses."

The engineer concluded his commentary and the director thanked him. The crew then turned their attention to someone from the exporters' association, who was getting ready to give his commentary on the situation.

Laafrit went over to the car with the engineer. They took off and didn't exchange a word until they got back to the café. During the ride, Laafrit thought about the vials he'd found at Bensallam's house. Should he give them to the engineer so he could analyze their contents? How embarrassed would he be if it turned out they contained some kind of folk Viagra, just like Detective Said said.

When they got out of the car, Laafrit gave his phone number to the engineer, who wrote it down in a small notebook. Si Lahsan then gave his number to the detective.

"Listen," said Laafrit, "there are some vials I found at Bensallam's house yesterday and I don't know what's in them."

He opened his car trunk and gave the box to the engineer.

"A detective from Beni Mellal said he'd seen these kinds of vials sold at the markets by herbalists, especially as a kind of folk aphrodisiac," he added, laughing.

The engineer smiled and looked at one of the vials.

"I'd be surprised if Bensallam didn't know about Viagra," he said.

The two laughed and shook hands.

"We'll stay in touch, right?" said Laafrit.

"Of course. Whatever the results are on the vials, I'll let you know."

"And I'll let you know what we find out in the case," said the detective.

Laafrit embraced the engineer warmly before finally heading back to Tangier.

12

AFTER HE GOT BACK FROM Beni Mellal, Laafrit tried several times to get in touch with Luis but was repeatedly thwarted by Luis's voicemail. Laafrit had to leave a short message telling him to call as soon as possible but Luis didn't get back to him for four days.

It was six o'clock on Saturday night. Laafrit had spent the entire day lying in bed reading the papers. He was surprised to find so many articles about the tomatoes. Some of them were terrifying and went so far as to say the price of tomatoes would increase many times over, even suggesting tomatoes might just gradually disappear from the markets. Another article declared: "May God have mercy on harira," and said Moroccans would have to come up with a different soup to break the fast for the upcoming Ramadan, one that didn't contain tomatoes. Laafrit was shocked as he read in another article that more than three million Moroccans lived on tomatoes as their main food source, and that only ten percent of Moroccans consumed the same grade of tomatoes that was exported to Europe. The other ninety percent were stuck with tomatoes of much lower quality. The same article mentioned Moroccan tomatoes had a place of honor on European tables, making them a point of competition and envy for growers in Israel and Spain, the two other major exporters of tomatoes. The reason for this was that Moroccan tomatoes were richer in nutrients and vitamins, thanks to the country's excellent geography, soil, and daily sun.

As he turned the pages, Laafrit paused for a while at a headline that read: "Has a Sabotage War Erupted against Moroccan Goods in Spain?" The paper reported that the police in Almería had opened a criminal investigation into a fire that broke out at dawn on Thursday at an agricultural factory used to pack fruits and vegetables coming from Morocco. The Spanish News Agency EFE quoted police sources saying that the investigation into the incident had begun because of suspicions that the fire was arson. Relying on a source from the fire department, it mentioned that the wooden pallets holding the crates of fruits and vegetables helped spread the flames, causing massive losses that hadn't been calculated yet. A source from the Association of Fruits and Vegetables stated that the incident had stirred up widespread anger among Almería produce dealers because of the strong possibility that the importation of agricultural products from Morocco would now be disrupted. The article also mentioned that about two weeks ago, groups of international truck drivers had blocked traffic to and from Morocco, causing heavy financial losses.

After reading the papers, Laafrit understood why he couldn't get hold of his friend Luis. Maybe he was in charge of the arson case.

When the phone rang suddenly, Laafrit was watching the news on the Spanish channel TVE. He didn't expect it to be Luis.

"My man, where are you?" asked Laafrit excitedly, turning down the TV.

"Stewing in tomatoes," said Luis, laughing.

"Anything new?" he asked, sitting up and pressing the receiver to his ear.

"How about we meet in fifteen minutes?"

"Where? In international waters?" asked Laafrit, laughing again.

"No, in Tangier. You'll find me waiting for you in the lobby of Hotel Shams."

"Even if you rent a private plane, you couldn't make it to Tangier in fifteen minutes," said Laafrit, annoyed.

"I'm already here," said Luis.

"Are you serious?" Laafrit asked in disbelief.

"Come on over to Hotel Shams and you'll see for yourself."

Laafrit still thought Luis was pulling his leg.

"If you're really in Tangier, why didn't you come to my house? You know where I live."

"Just meet me here at the hotel, okay?"

"I'll be right there," said Laafrit despite his suspicions.

He found Luis sitting in the hotel lobby with a pot of mint tea in front of him. Laafrit beamed as he embraced his friend warmly. They stood there for several moments, each holding the other's arm, smiling happily.

"It's great to see you!" Laafrit said in Spanish.

"How do I look after all this time?" asked Luis in Arabic.

"Looks like you've put on a pound or two, my friend. Been drinking a few extra cervezas, eh?"

Luis laughed and invited Laafrit to sit down.

"You've put on a bit too," said Luis. "But let's not talk about us. How are your wife and daughter?"

"Great. And you? You still haven't decided to get married?"

"You sound like my father!" asked Luis, smiling. "But if you can suggest a beautiful Moroccan girl, then why not?"

The waiter arrived, preventing Laafrit from responding. He ordered a pot of mint tea too. Laafrit scrutinized Luis's face and could see he was anxious to cut straight to the point.

"I read in a newspaper about a fire that broke out at a packing factory in Almería," said Laafrit.

Luis's green eyes widened.

"That's right," he said. "But that was last Thursday."

"Are you the primary on the investigation?" asked Laafrit.

"Yeah, because the case is connected somehow to Carlos. I've only slept a few hours in the past three days. Your dead men have taken me into a labyrinth I had no idea existed."

"Is that why you're here?" Laafrit asked.

"Yeah. And where've you gotten in your investigation?"

"I went to Beni Mellal and questioned the wife of Bensallam, the shooting victim. From there, I went to Oualidia in the Doukkala region, which Bensallam visited the last time he was here."

"What did you find out?"

"I've got some ideas," said Laafrit after a moment. "But I'd rather listen to the guy who came to town from the other side of the sea."

Luis took a sip from his glass and kept silent until the waiter brought Laafrit's tea.

"I've . . . brought . . . you . . . a . . . bombshell," said Luis, stressing each word and letting out a laugh. "So, let's begin with what we know for sure. The first thing is that Bensallam had his last meal with Carlos at Al Hamra Restaurant before he disappeared in Almería. It was salad, paella, and chocolate flan. He also had lots of red wine."

"Same meal found in his stomach during the autopsy," said Laafrit.

"Good," said Luis. "As for the three drowning victims, I confirmed with the guards at the Almería port that they recently spent a whole day cleaning Carlos's boat. Carlos's three sons—Juan, Antonio, and Gabriel—were with them. That night, they all set out on a fishing trip. Afterward, no trace was seen of the three Moroccans."

Laafrit was about to say something but Luis indicated with his hand that he shouldn't interrupt.

"You want to ask what happened to Bensallam and the three illegals on Carlos's boat. Good. The reason they went fishing that night was to take them out as close as possible to Moroccan waters opposite Tangier and toss them into the sea.

That way, their bodies would wash up on your side and you'd think they were harraga."

"But why Tangier?" asked Laafrit. "The Melilla coast is closer to Almería."

"Melilla," said Luis, "is considered Spanish territory, so very few harraga set out from there. The real harraga grave-yard is between Gibraltar and Tangier. Carlos and his sons tossed them out near Tangier so their bodies wouldn't wash up on Spanish shores. The reason for his precaution was that the shooting victim would have to be investigated. If Carlos hadn't had to shoot Bensallam, he would've thrown all four into the middle of the sea and been done with it."

"Why'd he shoot Bensallam then?" asked Laafrit anxiously.

"That guy was supposed to meet the same fate as his buddies, but after having dinner with Carlos he realized something was up and that he was being tricked. When they left the restaurant, Carlos told him they'd head down to the port to take a night fishing trip. But on the way, Bensallam figured out what Carlos had in store for him. He freaked out and told Carlos to pull over. Carlos did it, but before Bensallam could get out of the car, Carlos emptied four rounds into him. Carlos then put on Bensallam's jacket, zipped it up, and sat him upright in the car to make it look like he was still alive. From there, he headed down to the port and told his sons what happened. He had one of them take the three illegals to the port café, while Carlos and his other two sons got Bensallam's body out of the car and hid it in the boat. I think you know what happened next."

"What happened next," said Laafrit quickly, "is that the four were thrown into the sea opposite Tangier. But what's the motive?"

"You haven't even touched your tea yet!" said Luis, laughing.

Laafrit calmly poured some mint tea into his cup and took a quick sip.

"Before talking about the motive," said Luis, "you should know that Carlos Gomez is the biggest tomato farmer in Andalusia. He also owns the biggest agricultural exporting company in the region. Like I told you, he's an extreme racist. He thinks the 'Moors'—sorry for the word, Laafrit—are just a bunch of animals lower than human beings. He just doesn't get how a third-world African country can compete with him for the European markets. He sometimes says openly Spain should reoccupy the 'land of the Moors.' He thought it was a huge insult the fishing agreement between your country and mine wasn't renewed, especially since he has investments in the industry. He owns twenty boats that are now dry-docked because of that unsigned treaty."

"So he must be the one behind the fire that broke out at the packing factory in Almería," said Laafrit.

"Of course he was behind it. But I don't have anything I can convict him with. This case has put me in close contact with Carlos and his sons, and they're big-time racists, just like him."

They both paused to take a sip of tea.

"Why kill the four Moroccans?" asked Laafrit.

Luis took a deep breath and looked slyly around the lobby.

"After I confirmed Carlos's connection to the victims, I went back to the illegal immigrant camps on the outskirts of Almería and looked for Jaouad Benmousa. Let me tell you, this guy deserves all the credit for piecing together the puzzle."

Luis took a deep breath and a long sip from his cup. He savored the eager look in Laafrit's eyes.

"When I found him," he resumed, "I told Jaouad what had happened to his buddies. He asked me to take him to the nearest phone booth so he could call his family and the families of the other four to confirm the news. He was comfortable with me because I spoke to him in Arabic. After he talked to everyone, he told me he would've met the same fate if he'd gone along with his buddies. He said Carlos is the one who spread the rumor they went to Madrid. Jaouad was sure something terrible had happened to them but not something as bad as murder.

"He told me Bensallam, after he got back to Almería from his last trip to Morocco, was suffering from a serious crisis. He drank a lot and broke down in tears for no apparent reason. Once he hit his head against a wall, threatening to kill himself. Eventually, he told the others he was bent on destroying what he could of Carlos's tomatoes. The day before the murder took place, he confided in the other four from Beni Mellal what was tearing him apart. That secret, my friend, is the key to the case."

Luis scanned the lobby again as if he was afraid someone was watching them. He then leaned toward Laafrit.

"Carlos," he continued, "gave Bensallam a liquid chemical with a highly advanced and easily spreadable virus to wipe out the tomatoes in your country."

Laafrit stared at Luis in disbelief.

"I don't know how it was made," added Luis, "but the important thing is that it could wipe out a field of tomatoes with only a small quantity put into the irrigation ducts."

Laafrit instantly remembered the strange vials he found in Bensallam's house, the ones he had given to the agricultural engineer, Si Lahsan.

"Carlos picked Mohamed Bensallam for the job," said Luis. "That's why Carlos got him legal papers and gave him a ton of cash. He supplied Bensallam with the chemical and made a deal with him to demolish all the tomato fields in your country. But Bensallam, according to what Jaouad told me, didn't go through with it all the way. He stopped with Doukkala, brought what he had left of the chemical back to Almería, and hid it in his house."

"Because he regretted what he did?" asked Laafrit.

"Yes. As I told you, Jaouad said Bensallam was suffering from serious depression after he came back from Morocco the last time. Bensallam was on the verge of suicide but he found a way out with a crazy idea. He got his buddies from his neighborhood together and revealed to them the crime he had committed against his country. He told them he hadn't carried out the whole plan and that he kept most of the vials. He asked for their help in getting revenge against Carlos."

"So he wanted to destroy Carlos's fields with what he had left?" asked Laafrit in disbelief, swallowing with difficulty.

"Exactly," said Luis. "He asked his friends to help him and promised to split the rest of the money with them. Bensallam said they'd all go to Madrid afterward."

"But how'd Carlos find out?" asked Laafrit impatiently.

"The three sold Bensallam out to Carlos, wanting to get legal papers in exchange. As for Jaouad, he admitted to me he refused to go along with Bensallam's plan. Jaouad told him to destroy the rest of the chemical and forget the whole thing. But when Carlos found out what Bensallam had in mind, he immediately got his sons together and decided then and there to get rid of them all. Luckily for Jaouad Benmousa, the others didn't mention his name to Carlos, maybe because they thought it'd be easier to get papers for three instead of four. You know what happened next. They all wound up dead, washed up on your shores."

Laafrit kept quiet for a while.

"The whole thing's hard to believe, right?" said Luis, yanking Laafrit out of his silence.

"Bensallam didn't have any suspicions about his friends?" asked Laafrit. "He didn't try to flee?"

"Carlos didn't give him the chance. As soon as he found out what was going on, he made the three Moroccans think he'd get them papers by saying he'd make them his official employees. And to make it seem like he was serious, he sent them with his sons to the port to work on the boat. Meanwhile, Carlos searched Bensallam's house on the farm and found the rest of the vials. He then asked Bensallam to come out with him, and I've got eyewitnesses who saw Carlos with Bensallam at a number of places that day. The idea was to prevent Bensallam from going back to the farm so he wouldn't get suspicious his house had been searched. Later, Carlos took him to Al Hamra Restaurant, where they ate dinner together. On the way to the port, Bensallam realized something wasn't right and told Carlos to pull over. The result was the four shots. And just so you know, the gun Carlos owns is the same kind you found at Issa Karami's house."

"What are the odds!" said Laafrit, shaking his head. "How'd you find Carlos's gun?"

"After the fire broke out at the packing factory for fruits and vegetables from Morocco, I immediately thought of Carlos but I didn't have a good excuse to take him down to the station for questioning. But when I was going home last night, I saw his car parked in front of a popular bar in Almería and decided to search it. I pulled up and saw the door was unlocked. I took a quick look inside and found the gun in the glove compartment. Keep in mind, Carlos has a permit to carry a gun. What was unusual as far as I was concerned was that it was the same kind used to kill Bensallam. A Beretta nine-millimeter."

"Beautiful," said Laafrit. "But this chemical you talked about, where was it made?"

"I don't know," said Luis. "What I know is that Carlos has a daughter, Maria, who's married to a Spanish Jew, and they both now live in Israel. Her husband's a big tomato farmer, too. He owns an international company that exports tomato seedlings—"

"Carlos's company," said Laafrit, cutting him off, "is the one that acted as intermediary last year for a Moroccan farmer who imported Israeli seedlings called Daniella. These carried TYLCV, a virus spread by a tiny whitefly called *Bemisia tabaci*."

Luis let out a laugh as if he just heard a joke.

"Where'd you get that?"

"At the time," Laafrit went on, ignoring Luis's question, "Moroccan newspapers put all the blame on Israel and Spain without any proof. They thought Moroccan tomatoes were being sabotaged because Morocco's the largest competitor for your tomatoes and Israel's. The Moroccan press inflated the idea of a plot, which you know readers love, to boost their sales. But Israel suffered from the whitefly too, and they took serious precautions against exporting these seedlings. I'm thinking that the competitors were inspired by this to make the chemical."

Laafrit leaned back in his chair and closed his eyes for a moment.

"I think I've got some vials of the stuff," he said.

Luis's eyes widened. He leaned his elbow on the table and put his hand on his cheek, looking intently at Laafrit.

Laafrit told him the details of his trip south to Beni Mellal and how he had discovered the vials and the map of Doukkala. He then told Luis about going to Oualidia and questioning the agricultural engineer. When he said he left the vials with the engineer to run tests on them, Luis slapped himself on the cheek a number of times.

"You crafty devil, Laafrit!" he said enthusiastically. "If your engineer proves those vials really contain the chemical used to destroy the tomatoes, we'll have the material evidence to convict Carlos and his partners. Once we've got that, we'll unleash the scandal and newspapers around the world will put it on their front pages! It's such a stroke of good luck. Call your engineer right now and tell him to speed things up!"

Luis suddenly paused.

"Did you at least keep one of the vials?" he asked.

"Take it easy," said Laafrit. "A cop in Beni Mellal thought they probably just had a folk version of Viagra."

Luis let out a ringing laugh as Laafrit took out his cell phone and notebook. He looked for the engineer's phone number and dialed it. An automated message said the phone was out of network coverage. Laafrit put his cell down on the table between them.

"His phone's off," said Laafrit, with a nervous hint in his voice.

After such an excited conversation, a state of apprehensive silence hit the two as each was immersed in his thoughts.

"Strange," said Laafrit, with a hint of disbelief. "Imagine if these people had managed to destroy all of Morocco's tomatoes and others wiped out all the tomatoes in Spain and Israel. What would happen?"

"What would happen," said Luis, with the same sense of distress, "is that tomatoes would just disappear from the markets. At that point, these crooks wouldn't even find what they were competing for."

"There'd at least be oranges," said Laafrit sarcastically.

"They'd wipe those out too," said Luis, "in the name of competition, isolating markets, and preserving prices."

"And mad cow disease?" asked Laafrit with a shudder. "Maybe they're lying when they say it comes from cow fodder. Why couldn't there be some criminal act behind that too? Competition justifies everything."

"We're in the age of globalization and the new world order," said Luis, smiling in agreement and tapping his fingers on the table. "The globe isn't under the control of states or governments any more. Multinational companies rule the world now and soon they'll give way to lobbies and even criminal syndicates. Please, please, call your engineer friend."

Laafrit called again and got the same automated message. The phone was out of coverage.

"He's probably just stuck in the lab," said Luis.

"He said he'd call as soon as learns something," said Laafrit. "Look, you're my guest. What do you say we go back to my house?"

"Are you crazy?" Luis protested. "I didn't come all the way here just to see you, my friend. I came for Fifi's show!"

Laafrit let out a long laugh.

They ate dinner at the Pyramids, which gave Laafrit the chance to tell Nadia her ex-husband was now under investigation for failure to pay child support. After midnight, Laafrit and Luis went to Club East and sat at a table right in front of the dance floor. The place was dark and packed to the gills with groups of people at tables with bottles and glasses. As usual, Laafrit took a close look around and waited a while before taking his first sip. He seemed depressed and had a despondent look in his eyes.

Laafrit still couldn't stop thinking about the case. He realized how hard it would be to write the report for his bosses since the whole case still lacked corroborating evidence. Despite all his effort and help, Luis hadn't followed official procedure in his investigation. He hadn't brought any proof. The whole thing now rested on the agricultural engineer, Si Lahsan. And that was assuming he discovered the vials actually contained the chemical that destroyed the tomatoes. Then they'd easily have enough to get a conviction. And the front pages.

The musicians started warming up and the lights went out, indicating the second part of the evening was about to begin, the one reserved for Fifi's number. The MC presented her to the audience excitedly while striking a tambourine in his hand. Laafrit looked over at Luis and saw him covered in sweat.

Spotlights shone down on the dark dance floor as the musicians' pulsating rhythm leveled out and then suddenly stopped. After a few moments of dramatic silence, the drummer broke into a solo, cracking beats like a blazing fire. Fifi suddenly appeared, cutting nimbly across the dance floor with incredible turns. She got to the middle and an avalanche of light poured down on her. Her body shook in a feverish race with the drum. As the rhythm sped up, Fifi's hips shook so fast it seemed like she was being given electric shocks.

The opening number lasted only five minutes, after which the lights came on. Luis immediately stood up like a fool and began clapping wildly. When Fifi noticed him, her face lit up and she let out a sly laugh. At that exact moment, Laafrit's cell phone rang in his jacket pocket. He couldn't take the call in the middle of all the noise, so he made his way through the jammed tables toward the exit. When he answered, he heard the voice of a woman who sounded as if she was screaming.

"Detective Laafrit?"

"Yes," he answered, yelling over the surrounding noise. "Who's this?"

"Hosna, Si Lahsan's wife."

Laafrit could hear the woman's breathing interspersed with weeping.

"I'm waiting to hear from Si Lahsan. Where is he now?" Laafrit asked worriedly.

"They killed him!" Hosna yelled after a long silence. "My husband was killed! They shot him six times!"

Laafrit took a deep breath, trying to collect himself.

"Please calm down. How'd you get my number?"

"I found it in my husband's notebook. He told me about you."

"Where was your husband killed?"

"At the lab. He was conducting tests on the vials you gave him."

Laafrit's hand froze on his cell phone.

"What happened?" he asked.

"The killers took all the vials," she said, her voice cracking. "They burned the computer he was working on and left. What did you give to my husband? What was in those vials?"

She was so overcome by grief she couldn't go on. The line suddenly went dead. Laafrit was stunned at the news and realized he'd been incapable of expressing any kind of consolation. His first thought was that this woman would definitely blame him for what happened to her husband.

He needed some time to digest the disaster. He looked for a lozenge but he didn't have a single one. He turned to the closest person to him and asked for a cigarette. Laafrit just stood there, smoking it emotionlessly. He looked into the club and saw Fifi dancing around Luis with a charm and spirit that made him think she was dancing for him alone. He saw Luis suddenly jump out of his seat and begin dancing behind her, pretending to be a slave bound by chains and shackles. The crowd immediately broke out in cheers and applause.

Laafrit knew now wasn't the time to interrupt Luis. He made his way out of the club as a kind of constriction overwhelmed him. He almost fell over, collapsing on the ground. Once outside, he was about to pass out but he managed to get hold of himself and resist the nausea rising up in him. He left his car behind and started walking, filling his lungs with the cool moist air blowing in from the sea.

The streets were empty except for some staggering drunks. Laafrit watched one of them stumble forward and fall to the ground. The drunk fought hard to get up, but as soon as he did, he fell back down again. All the tragedies this country's living through are right there, Laafrit thought. We're just like this drunk who can't manage to stay upright.

By the time he reached the street where he lived, he'd walked aimlessly for a long time. It was about three in the morning. The walk had cleansed him somewhat of the blame he felt for the engineer's death.

Before he opened the door of his apartment building, he heard what he thought was the sound of yelling. He looked down the narrow street and saw a light coming from one of the apartments. He was amazed and couldn't stop himself from smiling when he realized he was hearing the teacher's husband apologizing to her for what he had done, crying and asking for forgiveness. The husband was observing the police order not to beat his wife. But, Laafrit thought, that's another case.